Deviled

Lake Erie Mysteries, Volume 2

Olivia Breen

Published by Olivia Breen, 2021.

DEVILED

First edition. February 21, 2021.

ISBN: 979-8201802554

Written by Olivia Breen.

Chapter One

and now for our feature presentation
pretty girls all in a row
it's almost time for the final show
walls of water floors of sand
drumroll please strike up the band
the time has come; put out the light
and soon two wrongs will make it right
goodbye my dears farewell adieu
the devil's bed is made for you

Chapter Two

He's mad that trusts in the tameness of a wolf, a horse's health,
a boy's love, or a whore's oath. *~King Lear*

I had just enough time to shriek and suck a huge gulp of air into my lungs before plunging to my certain death. My eyes were scrunched closed, yet tears of terror still managed to leak out and down my cheeks. My sweaty hands were swiftly losing their tenuous grip on the metal rail that was the only thing between me and the expanse of oppressive midsummer air beneath my feet.

I hadn't ridden a roller coaster in at least ten years, and of course, my best friend, June, insisted we sit in the front seat of the front car. Every time. Even though we had spent most of the morning riding every coaster in the amusement park, I still couldn't get past the feeling of impending death that clutched at my chest, threatening to stop my heart from beating. Less than a minute later, it was all over. I was still alive.

Back on terra firma, I took a moment, concentrating on calming my wobbly knees before I checked my watch. "June, our room has got to be ready by now. Let's check in with the guys at the dock and then head over to the hotel to register."

"Sure, Francie. That was the last coaster in the park anyway. I was starting to get bored."

"Seriously, June?" Before she could rethink and drag me off for round two, I turned and strode off in the direction of the marina located at the edge of the giant amusement park. Both the park and the marina were part of the world-famous Devil's Island Resort, the five-star complex on the shore of Lake Erie located just across Sandusky Bay from our own home port, Beacon Pointe.

It was the second day of July, and my husband Hammond and I had skimmed across the bay in our forty-foot sedan cruiser in anticipation of a fun-filled getaway. Our new friend, Detective Jack Morgan, and my longtime best friend, June, were our companions for the long weekend. Jack and June had been involved in a romantic relationship of sorts for the past month. He had come into all of our lives over the recent Memorial Day weekend on Kelleys Island when, thanks to the detective's expert skills, June and I narrowly escaped death by drowning at the hands of a psychotic killer. How romantic is that?

Nothing quite so dramatic was on tap for our July Fourth celebration. Our plan for this weekend was simple. I was registered for the three-day Drama Divas Workshop and Seminar taking place from July second through the fourth at the exclusive Devil's Island Resort Hotel. It would be a fun way to earn enough credits to keep my licensure up to date. The beauty of heading up the drama department at the local college was that I had my summers free to pursue other interests such as boating, shopping, and spending time at our summer condo. The irony of the conference title was not lost on any of us, since each of us wished for nothing more than a drama-free weekend. Our last holiday boat excursion had turned into the exact opposite of relaxing when we were drawn right into the middle of an arson and murder investigation.

June would be attending the conference as my guest. She could throw a little work into the mix too. As a freelance journalist, she always had a story percolating for one of the numerous magazines she wrote for. As a former investigative reporter, she kept her eyes and ears open for possible ne'er-do-wells trying to stir up trouble. Meanwhile, Jack had invited Hammond to be his golf partner at the annual Lake Erie Commerce Association's golf tournament taking place over the same three days. The guys planned to embark early in the morning for Sunset Marina, just up the coast, where they would enjoy a few days of manly golf fun. We would all reconnect on the evening of the final day of the seminar, Independence Day. According to the itinerary, the conference would wind up with a no-holds-barred mystery dinner theater featuring group participation and promises of noteworthy special effects. After dinner, we would kick back, have a few cocktails and enjoy the resort's grand fireworks display from the back of our boat. At least that was the plan.

I PUNCHED IN THE FOUR-digit code to open the iron security gate at the entrance of our assigned dock at Devil's Island Marina. I expected to find Hamm and Jack sitting on the dock debating the finer points of domestic versus foreign cigars and beer—a topic that never seemed to get old for them; but instead, the knot of people clogging the walkway blocked off all view of our boat slip. Squeezing and shimmying our way through the crowd caused my adrenaline to surge like I was dangling over the monstrous hill of the Daredevil once again.

"What the heck is going on, Francie? Did someone fall off a boat?"

"I have no clue. I can't see anything. Where did all these people come from?"

We managed to break free of the throng and found ourselves in the center of a captive audience. I expected to see blood or dismembered body parts or at least someone being held at gunpoint. I wasn't surprised, however, when I recognized Bob at the eye of the storm.

Bob was the resort's marina manager. He had been there for as long as anyone could remember and had been disliked by everyone he came in contact with for just as long. Bob was standing on the dock next to our boat with his hands folded over his protruding beer belly that his dingy, tank-style T-shirt could barely contain. His feet were bare, his cut-off jeans were riding dangerously low, and a tattered captain's hat was perched atop his bald head. None of this was out of the ordinary except for the sight of our friend Barb who was standing on the deck of our boat screeching at the top of her lungs and clutching her little shih tzu, Monster. The sound of her squeals rivaled the monthly tornado siren test that still managed to take me by surprise on the first Tuesday of every month. I looked from my husband to Jack and then to June hoping to telepathically figure out what was going on. When my psychic attempt at communication failed, I stepped onto the boat, grabbed Barb by the shoulders, and yelled, "Shut up!"

The ensuing silence was deafening. Barb stood there, mouth still open in mid-screech, but everything was quiet. Now was my chance to get a word in. "What in the name of Shakespeare's ghost is going on here?"

Just as quickly as Barb had quieted, she began her tirade again. Thankfully it was a few decibels lower and almost coherent this time.

"My babies! He tried to kill my babies." As if on cue, Monster let out a little squeak. Then from beside me, a double-bass "woof" reverberated around the cockpit. I hadn't noticed Barb's other baby, Ogre, the St. Bernard, lying under the table. For a 200-pound dog, Ogre could make himself unobtrusive and almost small.

Upon hearing Ogre's booming greeting, June leapt onto the boat and landed in a crouch next to her canine friend. She has always had a weakness for big, drooling, goofy animals. Her fondness, however, did not extend to big, drooling, goofy men. After inspecting her furry friend for evidence of harm, she faced off with Bob and demanded in a steely voice to know what he had done.

Bob stood on the dock chewing on an unlit cigar with a look of utter boredom on his face. When it was apparent that he was not going to answer, Barb began her story from the beginning.

"This man is the devil. I left my boat for just over an hour so I could run into the park to buy some souvenirs for my grandkids and Bob tried to kill my babies."

"What did he do, Barb? They look fine to me."

"He unplugged my electrical cord so he could suck up to some fancy speed boat owner who had a crew of barely dressed bimbos on board. He put them in the slip beside my boat and then gave them my outlet since they have two air conditioners on board and apparently needed my power as well as theirs to keep themselves comfortable. It's almost 100 degrees today, and the dogs were left to cook in the cabin with no air conditioning. If Hamm and Jack hadn't noticed them barking and rescued them, they would have died."

"Is this true Bob?" June was now back on the dock and so close to the repulsive man that his slobbery cigar stub was the only thing separating their faces.

"What's the big deal? They didn't die did they? This broad is just hysterical. Maybe it's that time of the month."

There was no more discussion. I knew what that look on June's face meant. Like a panther pouncing on some small prey, June lunged forward, hooked her leg around Bob's right knee, and with just the slightest shove sent him plunging into the water. His captain's hat and soggy cigar floated to the surface first. Then the rest of Bob surfaced like so much scum from a slimy pond. Green algae dripped from his bald head as he got his feet under him and stood armpit deep in the shallow water. No one made a move to assist him. A few cheers went up from the thinning crowd. The excitement had come to an end, and the audience moved on to to find alternate amusements.

"Are you nuts, woman? You could have killed me!"

"What's the big deal? You didn't die, did you? I think you're just being hysterical." With that said, June came back aboard and settled into the corner of the bench seat to watch as Bob struggled to disentangle himself from his seaweed net and get back to dry land. Monster took a flying leap out of Barb's vice grip landing comfortably in June's lap, while Ogre readjusted his head to place it on her feet. Juniper Julia Augusta, defender of dogs, held court over her new loyal subjects.

Chapter Three

If after every tempest come such calms/ May the winds blow till they have waken'd death! *~Othello*

The sky had a purplish tinge to it and was darker than usual for this time of year. I made a mental note to check the weather report. Summer storms had a way of popping up on the lake with almost no warning. Hamm beat me to it. "According to NOAA Weather, there's a chance of a pop-up storm tonight, but the radar isn't showing anything ominous for the next few hours. I think we have time for some chips and a beer before we leave you two ladies to your weekend of fun."

Barb gathered up her doggie duo and headed back to her own boat, satisfied that Bob was no longer a threat. I uncapped three Corona Lights and a Bud Lite (since Jack refused to drink beer that required the addition of fruit) and passed them all around. We raised our bottles and toasted June for finally giving Bob a taste of his own medicine. Even Hamm, who usually disapproved of June's outrageous outbursts, couldn't hide the smile of approval that tugged at the corners of his lips.

"For once, I can completely relate, June. That guy has no redeeming qualities. Last August, I was trying to dock here on a windy day. Francie was on the bow ready to toss him a line, and do you know what that jerk did? Nothing. He stood on the dock with his hands in his pockets. Francie nearly fell off the boat, and the hull got a nice dent where it hit the dock post."

"I remember that," I interjected. "He said something like 'Be sure to stop in the office to pay for dockage as soon as you get your lines tied.' I couldn't believe his nerve. He just strolled down the dock and didn't offer us any help at all. What an ass."

We told a few more "Why we hate Bob" stories while we finished up our drinks, but the moment the last chip was out of the bowl, both June and Hamm jumped up and began to move things along. The only thing my husband and my best friend have in common is the inability to sit still for an extended period of time. Before I got to the lime at the bottom of my beer bottle, I was kissing my husband goodbye and being dragged toward the resort by June.

Since we had had the good sense to have the men deliver our suitcases to the resort earlier, we were able to go straight to the convention registration and reception without the burden of luggage. A quick stop in the elegantly appointed ladies' restroom to freshen up our lipstick and fluff our hair took all of five minutes. The remainder of the registration process was a bit more complicated.

"Just choose one June. It's not like this is a matter of life and death."

"I know, but I love dressing up, so "Theatrical Makeup Design and Application" sounds really fun. On the other hand,

"Improvisation: Comedy on the Fly," is right up my alley. Why do we have to choose only one?"

"Unless you can find a workshop on cloning yourself, you have to choose just one. They are both held at the same time. How about we go with set design? It might be fun to spend some time in the theater. I hear it's quite impressive."

"Okay, that sounds good. I'm already quite skilled at makeup and cracking jokes, so it couldn't hurt to learn a new skill. Why didn't you just say that from the beginning? We're missing out on free drinks. Come on."

My eye roll went unnoticed by June, but it did make me feel a little better. I signed us up for the 9:20-12:00 set design workshop that included scale renderings, then let myself be dragged along to the bar. Our lanyard-style name badges included four free drink tickets to be used throughout the weekend. I handed over ticket number one to the bartender/ mime, who with an exaggerated bow and a flourish, exchanged it for a glass of red wine.

We found a high-top table where we could set our glasses down, soak up the atmosphere, and people-watch. I recognized a few acquaintances from different conventions I had attended over the years as well as several drama-department heads from neighboring universities with whom I occasionally work. We exchanged friendly nods and waves as they made their way across the room, everyone trying to impress and work on connections. I was more interested in the tall blond woman who was stopping at each table for a moment or two.

"Do you recognize that woman, June? She looks like she might be an actress."

"Whoa, she looks like Angelina Jolie, but with blond hair. I don't think it's her, but I sure wouldn't mind if Brad dropped in for a guest appearance."

"Good day ladies. You've got the Angelina part right, but the last name is DeVille. I couldn't help overhearing your comment and I'm flattered. My name is Angelina DeVille, and I'm the manager of Devil's Island Resort and Conference Center."

"It's so nice to meet you. I thought for sure you were a famous surprise guest." My flattery didn't seem to phase her or cause her to conjure up a fake emergency to escape our close scrutiny. She simply gestured to the nearest waiter who immediately came to our table, efficiently set three glasses of rose champagne in front of us, then, without a word, melted back into the sea of socializing guests.

Ms. DeVille lifted her glass and waited for us to each select an elegant flute filled with pale pink bubbles. "I would like to propose a toast. It's more of an apology, actually. I heard that the two of you had an ugly run-in with my brother-in-law, Bob, this afternoon. I would like to sincerely apologize for his behavior on behalf of the resort and assure you that it is my main objective for the two of you to have a memorable and wonderful time for the rest of your stay here on our island."

"Boy, word travels fast around here, but I'll drink to that." We clinked our glasses together and took a sip of the delicious champagne. "That's very kind of you Ms. DeVille."

"Please, call me Angelina. And it's the least my husband and I can do to make up for Bob's dreadful behavior. He is a constant thorn in the side of this resort, but unfortunately because of his birthright, we're unable to get rid of him or even reprimand his atrocious behavior. I would like you both to come up to my suite after the reception for some refreshments and to pick up the all-access passes that we arranged for you. They will allow you free access to all park amenities, complimentary food and beverages at all resort eateries, and even full use of the hotel spa services. We're in the penthouse suite. Stop by any time after you've settled in. You'll need this code in the elevator to reach the top floor. There's a keypad beside the floor number." She scribbled a few digits on a napkin and handed it to me. With that, Angelina merged effortlessly back into the crowded room, and June and I were left staring at each other, confusion and delight on both our faces. June spoke first, "Did she say complimentary food and beverages?"

"I believe she did. Who would have thought that finally getting to dump Bob overboard would come with the added benefit of all-access resort passes. Well-played, June."

"Let's finish these drinks and go to our room to freshen up before we head up to the penthouse. Maybe they left us some complimentary snacks." In true June fashion, she was already rushing toward the lobby before I even set my glass down.

"Check out this room Francie. I should dump people in the lake more often."

"I agree. This is quite lavish. I can't see how Bob, acting like Bob, has caused all of this extravagance. I'm not complaining though. Let's unpack and change our clothes. Then we can get up to that suite before Angelina changes her mind."

"Cheers to that, Drama Diva. Now how do we decide which one of us is wearing this magnificent scarf and who gets the hip hat? We need to make an impression, I think."

"I've got dibs on the hat. Look at my hair. After all those rides today, I don't think I can get a comb through it, and there's no time to wash it and start over."

"It's a deal. I think I'll accessorize with some of the silver jewelry your sister loaned us from her Silpada business. I want to make a statement."

I checked out June's look: She had chosen a black tank top, black skinny jeans and black heels that probably cost more than my monthly mortgage payment, topped off with enough silver to give Fort Knox a run for its money. And then there was the scarf. June had wrapped the length of shimmery gray, taupe, and beige fabric loosely around her neck and let the ends fall to below her knees. It totally worked.

I left my curly hair down and arranged the black fedora I scored at a trade show discount sale on top of my head at just the right angle. The "barely flawed" Manolo Blahniks I acquired on eBay, a little black dress, and a great pair of black-and-silver dangley earrings completed my ensemble.

After appraising ourselves one last time and appropriately admiring each other's impeccable fashion sense, we grabbed our handbags and made our way to the elevator for the short ride up to the penthouse. I'm not a fan of tight enclosed spaces, but when I caught a glimpse of our reflection in the mirrored elevator walls, I had to smile. We were indeed an impressive pair—from June's cropped platinum hair and my shoulder-length, dark corkscrews to her tiny patent leather clutch and my cavernous black suede hobo bag, we both had it going on.

Chapter Four

Desire of having is the sin of covetousness. *~Twelfth Night*

The letter P above the door lit up, and the little ding announced we had arrived. The door slid open, and we stepped into the hall. My right ankle wobbled a bit as my heels sunk into the plush gray carpet of the hallway. It was a far cry from the flat, generic floor covering on the rest of the hotel levels, but it didn't take long to get acclimated to the luxurious environment and strut our stuff down the long corridor to the only door at the end of the hall.

I was just about to knock when the door flew open and a young girl hurled herself out of the room, careening toward us and barely avoiding a head-on collision. She didn't stop to apologize or to chat, which would have been impossible anyway since she was sobbing pitifully as she charged past us, down the hall, past the elevator, and into the stairwell.

"What the heck was that?"

"I don't have a clue," I replied. "Do you think we should leave? Maybe this isn't a good time for a social visit."

Before June could comment, a second figure appeared in the doorway.

"Won't you come in ladies? I apologize for that little scene. It wasn't nearly as bad as it looked, I assure you."

It doesn't happen often, but I admit, I was speechless. The person who had just addressed us was beyond Brad Pitt, even borderline Heathcliff. Thankfully, June stepped up to the plate and extended her hand.

"Hi. I'm sorry. We must have the wrong room. We were looking for Angelina DeVille. I'm June and this is Francie."

"Of course you are. We were expecting you. Again, I apologize for that little scene. I'm Damien, Angelina's husband. Won't you come in?"

June and I gave each other the "here we go" look and graciously accepted the darkly handsome man's invitation to step over the threshold into the world of the rich and possibly famous.

Angelina stood up from her seat by the expanse of glass overlooking the sparkling lake. The sun had briefly peeked out from behind the gathering clouds and was just starting its westward journey toward the horizon creating a backdrop of luminous color. She was wearing a long dress of shimmering honey-colored silk, nearly the exact shade of her waist-length hair, and standing there in front of the window, surrounded by the soft glow from outside, it was easy to imagine how ancient civilizations would have worshipped a sun goddess. Glancing at June and then down at my own black-on-black ensemble, I got the sinking feeling that if we got too close to her we might cause a solar eclipse.

"Please, please, come in. I'm so glad you came." Angelina gestured toward the sofa across from her chair. "Make yourselves at home. Help yourself to a little something to eat or drink."

Between the couch and the two chairs now occupied by Mr. and Mrs. DeVille, was an elegant cherry-wood coffee table laden with plates of crackers and cheese, and we weren't talking Ritz and Kraft Singles. Two open bottles of wine, a Pinot Noir and a Chardonnay, completed the inviting repast.

June and I sat across from the stunning couple and helped ourselves. After all, we didn't want to seem rude. I chose a glass of the red, and June loaded her little plate with as many fancy crackers and exotic cheese wedges as it could hold. I was mentally trying to tick off the events of the day that led us to this beautiful penthouse suite while sipping my drink, when Damien reached across the table and set two gold-trimmed glossy red cards in front of us. "Please accept our heartfelt apologies once more for the deplorable behavior of my brother, Roberto."

"Who the heck is Rober..."

I nudged June in the ribs and surreptitiously coughed "Bob" into my elbow. Printed on the front of the cards in gold letters were the words "Devil's Island VIP." On the back was listed in tiny print all of the venues, eateries, services, and attractions to which the passes allowed the holders free and unrestricted access. Near the bottom of the card, I spotted the name of the world-renown spa, Heaven's Gate. This conference was getting better and better by the minute thanks to the obnoxious, thorn-in-the-side, black sheep of the DeVille family. Who'd a thought.

The four of us chatted for a few minutes, we complementing the couple on the vast resort complex with offerings for absolutely everyone, and they asking questions about the drama conference and our plans for the next few days. When the topic of the marina came up, we all shifted a little uncomfortably in our seats.

I tried to skim over the topic, "My husband and I have been bringing our boat over here for years and always manage to have a wonderful time."

"Don't worry," Angelina said. "I know what you must be thinking. You have a good time as long as you don't need to go into the marina office for anything while Bob is on duty."

Being a competent journalist, June was adept at steering awkward conversations in new directions. "So, Damien, there can't be too many people around here with that name. I saw that tonight's feature at the dinner theater is Damien the Magnificent, Magician Extraordinaire. Could it be? Is it you?"

Damien stood up and took a theatrical bow. "At your service m'lady. Perhaps you would care to join me on stage tonight for a special performance?"

"Oh, I'm honored," June replied, "but I'd rather take notes and try to figure out your sleight of hand; Francie, however, is a born performer. She'd be perfect, I'm sure."

"If you don't mind," I added, "I'd love to play magician's assistant for an evening. It sounds intriguing."

"I look forward to it then. Now if you ladies will excuse me, I need to prepare for tonight. Adieu." He took his leave with a flourish, disappearing through one of the suite's doors which I assumed was his office or bedroom, and it seemed like a good time for us to depart as well.

"Angelina, it's been so nice getting to know you and your husband. Your hospitality is really above and beyond the call of duty, but we appreciate your generosity and plan to take in as much as we possibly can while we're here. See you tonight."

"Yes," June agreed, "and thanks again for the VIP cards."

"I'm delighted that you came up. There will be a table right up front reserved for you this evening. I look forward to seeing you at dinner."

June reached out to shake Angelina's hand, but just then, Angelina turned, bumping into June's other hand, the one still hanging onto her wine glass. It caught her off guard. The glass tipped, but June made a great save. Rather than splashing her beverage all over the DeVille's designer couch, she poured it down the front of her clothes, soaking her pretty scarf.

"No worries. At least I was drinking chardonnay. You can't even see it." June was being very magnanimous. After all, it was my scarf.

"Please, I insist you leave it with me. I'll have it cleaned and delivered to your room."

Angelina wouldn't take no for an answer, so June untied the length of silky fabric from around her neck and handed it to our host.

Angelina walked us to the door and our visit was complete. We got about halfway down the plush corridor, congratulating ourselves on the success of our little trip, and how lucky we were to make friends with the owners of the resort, when the heel of my designer footwear got snagged in the carpet again, and I stepped right out of it, never missing a stride. Well, that was better than doing a faceplant since I didn't really want to test my theatrical make-up skills just yet. I got down on my knees and was tugging on the shoe when we heard loud angry voices, familiar voices, coming from behind the door we had just closed behind us.

"Listen Angie, just let me take care of this. I guarantee that we won't be cleaning up these messes again. I've got it handled, and if any trouble comes down on me..."

The plush, shoe-eating carpet finally gave up my heel, and momentum rocketed me straight onto my back in the middle of the hall.

The doorknob of the penthouse turned, and I had to make a quick recovery, rolling over and getting myself upright. June and I scrambled toward the elevator so we could avoid being accused of eavesdropping. We stumbled into the mirrored elevator just as Damien crashed through the door of the suite shouting back at Angelina to let him take care of their little problem. June stabbed at the close button, and seconds before the steel doors met, Damien's piercing stare connected with my own. The indicator light for the lobby couldn't have come on fast enough.

"What the heck just happened Francie? That guy went from Don Draper charming to Norman Bates scary in the blink of an eye."

"I don't know, but I'm glad we got out of there when we did. I hope Angelina is all right."

June frowned. "What do you think Damien meant about 'handling their problem?' Was he talking about that hysterical employee, or Bob, or maybe us? He seemed furious."

"I don't know. It could be anything. We should probably leave it alone."

Before June could reply, her phone interrupted, chirping an alert signal. She flipped open her clutch to retrieve it and read the message on the screen. "It's a severe weather alert."

My first thought was Hamm. "We should run over to the marina to warn the guys in case they haven't heard the update. This afternoon, he said any bad weather wasn't supposed to roll in until overnight. Hamm hasn't responded to any of the recent texts I've sent him. His phone might be dead."

The elevator glided to a stop on the lobby level and the doors slid open to an empty hall.

"Oh no, not again. You have got to get that man a backup phone charger this Christmas so you aren't always worrying."

June pulled her phone out of her tiny handbag again and checked it for missed messages. "I haven't heard from Jack since we left the marina either. You're right. Let's head over to make sure they got the latest weather update. If both of their phones are off, they probably haven't heard the new forecast yet."

"That settles it. Plus, a brisk walk will help burn off all of that fancy wine and cheese so we'll have room for dinner."

Chapter Five

Go wisely and slowly. Those who rush stumble and fall.
~*Romeo and Juliet*

I followed June through the lobby and into the revolving exit door, mindful of where I placed my feet. I was more skilled than most at walking in high heels, but I didn't need to get my heel trapped in a door that never stopped turning. In the short time it took us to get outside, the sun had retreated for good and its radiant glow had been replaced by dark swirling clouds in a sky the color of eggplant and green olives. We picked up our pace and headed purposefully down the sidewalk in the direction of the marina. Once inside the iron gate, it was apparent that the boating community was prepping for a storm. All the boats were battened down, lawn chairs and grills were stowed, and the weekend vacationers, children, and pets had all retreated to safety inside their vessels. Except for Hamm and Jack. I didn't know if they were safe inside or not. The boat was not in the slip. Barb's boat was gone as well.

A bolt of lightning split the ominous clouds followed by exploding thunder, and then the sky opened up and the rain poured down.

I had to shout over the wind, rain, and thunder. "Come on June, we have to get out of this weather. Let's try the office."

The rain was relentless, and thunder and lightning didn't even wait their turns, flashing and booming right over each other. I reached the office door first and tried the handle.

"It's locked. What do we do now?"

"Run for it!"

A deafening clap of thunder punctuated June's sentence like an exclamation mark. We kicked off our fancy shoes and ran barefoot in the direction of the resort. The walking path was already flooding and we kicked up spray like kids racing through shallow water at the beach. The hotel was just up ahead silhouetted in the dark sky by flashes of lightning. And then everything went black. All the power on the island went out, and we were engulfed in shadows and darkness. The unfamiliar surroundings, the shadows mixed with blinding flashes of light was disorienting. We had to slow down to get our bearings.

My eyes were starting to adjust. "I think the hotel entrance is just up ahead. Come on. Let's get out of this downpour."

"I'm with you, Francie. Let's get to dry land."

Rain pelted my face like tiny shards of glass. We huddled together pushing our way through the wind until the revolving door was in reach. June gave it a shove but it wouldn't budge. The power outage had immobilized the door, so we had to make our way a little further down the walkway to a service entrance which had a non-motorized swinging door. I pulled it open, and we practically blew right into the lobby. Emergency lights were beginning to flicker as the generator kicked on. There was just enough light to see our way to the main stairwell.

June leaned heavily against the stairway entrance door. A puddle was forming around her feet. "Should we get our hike on and and walk the twelve flights or wait it out here until the power comes back on?"

"Let's do it. I'm freezing."

"Stairs it is then. Make sure to record these points in your Weight Watchers log. This is going to be an unscheduled calorie buster."

"Joke now my friend. Your metabolism will crash eventually, and you'll be asking me for advice."

"Okay. Sorry. Come here and help me push. I can't get the door open. Something is blocking the way."

We both put our shoulders to the door and shoved. It gave about an inch but that was it. I tried to imagine what could be behind the door that could be big enough and heavy enough to barricade our entrance to the stairwell.

"Just push, Francie." June was peering through the tiny opening into the blackness on the other side. "It looks like a big canvas bag probably overstuffed with somebody's dirty laundry."

"Well let's do this," I said. "On the count of three..."

"Wait. *On* three or after? I'm never sure."

I rolled my eyes. "One, two, then push."

"Got it. One...two..."

We shoved. The jammed door sprung open, and we barrelled through the opening, landing in a pile at the foot of the stairs. The large canvas bag that had apparently been propped against the door, flopped over and thudded against the floor and out of our path. I only hesitated a moment before hitting the stairs all-out, determined to prove to June that I still had it in me. "Come on, June. We're going to catch pneumonia if we don't get dry soon."

Huffing and puffing, we finally attained the holy grail of floor twelve. I had barely enough energy left to get the door open and make a beeline for the bed. I flopped my wet self across the covers and took a few deep breaths while my heart rate normalized. June made her way directly to the bathroom, and turned on the shower. Five minutes later, she emerged from the steamy room cocooned in a white, fluffy, bathrobe and matching towel wound around her head.

It was my turn. There was plenty of hot water, even with the back-up generator providing our electrical power. There were also plenty of plush towels and another complimentary robe. The teeth-chattering, underwear-soaking misadventure was quickly receding into my memory bank. Good riddance. I sat back down on the pillow-top queen bed and watched June reapply her makeup. "I think we're getting too old for this kind of vacation," I mused while fluffing my hair with my fingers.

"Now don't go getting all dramatic, Francie. It was just a summer storm. They do happen here on the islands. Regularly, I might add."

"I know, but after Memorial Day, I'm just a bit leery of coincidental disappearances. That empty boat slip spooked me. I'm not going to lie."

"Well, you have a point my friend, but this time I assure you that there is nothing to worry about. Hamm and Jack got the weather alert from the rest of the people at the docks and decided to leave so they could beat the storm. And men being men, they just forgot to tell us. I'm sure they thought we were already elbows deep in some dramatic nonsense seminar and wouldn't even notice they had left."

I knew that what June said made perfect sense, but just to be on the safe side, and to ease that little voice of doubt trying to grab my attention, I spilled the contents of my handbag onto the bed, extracted my phone, and pressed Hamm's number. He answered on the first ring.

"Hi, Honey. Is everything okay?"

"I'm fine but I was a little worried about you. I tried calling you earlier, but it went right to voicemail. June and I just got caught in a torrential downpour here. We went to the marina to see if you guys had gotten the weather update, but when we got to the boat slip, it was empty."

"Everything is fine, Francie. Barb got the weather alert, and one look at the sky told us we had better move quickly. We made it to Sunset Marina and got the boat tied up just as the storm hit. We're at the club house having dinner."

"Well, that's good. I feel better now. Promise me you'll plug your phone back in when you finish dinner and return to the boat. I'm guessing you don't have a lot of battery power. You're always forgetting to keep that thing charged."

"Yes, Francie, I promise. I love…"

And with that I lost the call. I'm sure he had charged his phone for all of about five minutes. For a smart, successful attorney, sometimes I wondered how he managed.

June had a bemused "I told you so" look on her face, but didn't rub it in. I felt better knowing that the guys were safe and enjoying themselves. I just wished I had had the chance to tell Hamm about our meeting with the DeVilles and our good fortune of scoring all the freebies. He would have gotten a kick out of knowing Bob's bad attitude had resulted in such good luck for us.

Now it was time to get back to the matter of our evening plans.

"Are we really going to get dressed again and go to the dinner show? It's probably been cancelled since the power went out."

As if on cue, the lights came back on, and I blinked while my eyes adjusted to the brightness of the room. I didn't recall turning on every light switch in the place, but I guess between the two of us, we had managed to do just that. So far, we were not being very conscientious stewards of the environment. Oh well. "I guess the show must go on. It won't take me long to get ready. We sure don't have anything else to do tonight, and we don't have to go outside again to get to the theater. Let's take the DeVilles up on their offer for those VIP seats at the magic show."

"Why not? I'll make some coffee while you get ready."

Chapter Six

All the world's a stage, /And all the men and women merely players; /They have their exits and their entrances, And one man in his time plays many parts. *~As You Like It*

The dinner theater was located on the main floor just down the hall from the check-in desk. We entered through the doors under the sign marked Crystal Theater. Wow. It was nothing less than magnificent. Crystal chandeliers glowed and sparkled with amber light. White pillar candles flickered on every table infusing the tiered room with a fairy tale quality. Two handsome ushers dressed in impeccable tuxedos appeared at the entrance at the exact time we did, and without missing a beat, gallantly escorted us by the elbow down the stairs to a row of plush booths positioned at the front of the theater facing the stage. Angelina and Damien were already seated in the center booth engaged in friendly-sounding conversation. Our hostess rose to greet us. "Welcome Francesca, June. I'm so glad you made it. I hope the storm and the power outage didn't cause you too much inconvenience." She extended her hand, indicating our places in the booth.

Our escorts bowed and took their leave while Damien got us settled in our seats across from him and his beautiful wife. He filled four glasses from a bottle of champagne that had been chilling in an ice bucket beside the booth and settled confidently into his seat. There was no sign of the furious man we had encountered at the elevator.

Angelina held her sparkling champagne flute out to us and offered a toast.

"May we never regret this. Cheers!"

We raised our glasses, clinked them around the table, and sipped. Glancing sideways at June, I tried to gauge her reaction to Angelina's unconventional toast, but she either didn't notice or didn't think it was all that unusual. Waiters in sharply-pressed uniforms arrived and silently orchestrated a dinner event fit for heads of state: buttered rolls and a delicate summer salad lightly tossed with a tangy vinaigrette, followed by filet mignon and lobster. The asparagus with cream sauce would surely have had Hammond offering his first-born child (or in our case, children—we have twins) in exchange for the recipe. Raspberry sorbet and mint cheesecake were the perfect finale to this production. Devil's Island was living up to its marketing blurb to be a place to give in to your wildest desires. As we made our way through each delicious course, I listened attentively as Damien explained the magic trick I would be participating in shortly.

"It sounds simple enough, but let me make sure I have it all down. I wouldn't want to spoil your show, Damien."

"No worries, Francie. This is child's play. I've done it hundreds of times."

Since I had done it zero times, I still wanted to run through the details. "So, first you will be selecting me "randomly" from the crowd to come on stage. I will then be assisted into the box where I will lay down with my head and feet sticking out each end. Then, after some interaction with the crowd, you will begin to saw the box in half. So far, so good?"

"That's right, Francie. The top of the box is solid, but once I get through the first inch, the saw will hit the trigger for the false bottom to drop out so your midsection can drop below the box. Then the saw goes the rest of the way through while you use your best acting skills to make it look really painful."

I caught myself unconsciously waving my hands and wiggling my toes, excited to be part of the magic. "And then presto! Once I've convinced the crowd that I have been cut in two, you remove the blade and the false bottom pops back into place and I am once again whole."

"Exactly."

"I just have one more question."

"Of course, what is it?"

"Has anyone ever actually been cut in half?"

Angelina and Damien burst into laughter and assured me that they had performed this trick repeatedly with no bloodshed. Their lighthearted attitude succeeded in putting me at ease. Almost. The lights blinked off and then on. This time it wasn't due to another power outage. Instead, it was a signal the show was about to begin. Damien excused himself to get to the stage, and I finished off the last drops of my champagne. In spite of myself, I was feeling a bit nervous.

June wished me luck and slid out of the booth so she could move around more freely with her camera, Damien began the show with some amazing illusions, and I admired the work of the light and sound technicians who were doing a great job setting the mood. It was apparent that nothing was short of first class at this resort.

Damien introduced his next illusion, explaining to the audience that an unsuspecting woman from the audience would be sawed in half. Angelina took my damp hand in her cool smooth grasp and gave it a squeeze for luck. Damien "randomly" selected me from the volunteers who wanted to participate in the illusion. I took a deep breath, stood up, and made my way to the stage entrance. June was at the opposite end of the stage giving me a thumbs up. I was about to return the gesture when I noticed a waitress tap her shoulder and hand her a highball glass. I couldn't tell for sure, but it looked like the girl who had been in the penthouse suite before we had arrived. If it was in fact her, she had pulled herself together, and there was no sign of her earlier tears. But right now, it was time for me to focus on my performance.

Damien reached out and helped me onto the stage, enthusiastically explaining to the audience what he was about to do. Meanwhile, two assistants directed me into the coffin-like wooden box positioned under a beam of light at center stage.

The stage lights blinded me since I had no other choice but to stare up into them while lying flat on my back in my wooden sarcophagus. Damien continued setting up our illusion, playing to the crowd, but I couldn't make out his words. All the outside sounds echoed around me, disorienting me further. I tried to look calm and cool and follow the show even though I could barely move my head. My eyes darted from side to side, and my legs were starting to cramp up, and I realized it was too late to rethink this whole gig. Just then a shadow blocked the bright light from my eyes, leaving me to stare up at the imposing figure looming over me. My eyes fixated on the gleaming blade of the saw in Damien's hand as it made its way toward my belly.

A hush had settled over the audience. All eyes were on me while my eyes sought reassurance from the darkly handsome sorcerer who held my life in his hands. Damien's steely gaze was anything but comforting. The expression on his face confused me. Was he in a trance? I sure hoped he was in control of the razor sharp blade he was drawing back and forth across the top of the wooden box that held me prisoner. I felt an icy shiver creeping its way down my spine. The blade sliced through the wood and I instinctively sucked in my gut in anticipation of its impending contact. The trigger should have been activated by this point. Something was wrong, and I needed to get out. "Stop! Please stop! Let me out of here!"

There was a collective gasp from the audience. The action on stage was riveting, but I was not acting. I was panicking. The saw sliced through the top of the box and still nothing gave way beneath me. I tried pushing down on the bottom of the box with what little body weight I could leverage considering all I had to work with was my torso. Still nothing. Damien continued sawing. I didn't want to spoil the illusion, but this was getting too close for comfort. I felt the vibration and added pressure as the gleaming steel blade made a first cut into the protective board placed directly on my stomach as a final layer of protection in case of an equipment malfunction. Damien the Magnificent, Magician Extraordinaire, didn't seem to notice though as he continued pulling the razor-edged saw blade back and forth across the last half inch of protection I had before being sliced in two.

That was it. My fight or flight instinct kicked in, and since flight was not an option, I had only one choice. "Stop, Damien. Stop! Something's gone wrong!"

I screamed and begged, alternating between fury and terror, but my protests had no effect. His expression never changed, and the saw never stopped. How good an actress did he think I was? I realize that the show must go on, but this was over and above any actor's commitment to the craft. I sucked in a huge breath and screamed, "Ham and eggs!" then squeezed my eyes shut waiting for the tearing pain that would surely follow.

Was I conscious or was I dreaming? At this point, I didn't know or care. I felt rather than saw a whirlwind of activity around my head. Finally, I dared to peek my eyes open. There was June, pushing her way through a gathering crowd and throwing herself at Damien so she could wrestle the saw from him and stop the blade from reaching its intended destination. Thank god she had recognized the code words we had established in case of emergencies; although I had never expected to actually need them.

Chapter Seven

Suspicion always haunts the guilty mind. *~King Henry VI*

Back in our hotel room, I was lying on the bed with a warm washcloth on my forehead. June was pacing at the foot of the bed, organizing her own thoughts about the evening. She asked me the same questions I was trying to work out for myself.

"What happened tonight? I thought you had this all under control, Francie. I didn't think you were in any real danger until you shouted 'Ham and Eggs.' It took me a second to realize what was going on since I hadn't even thought about that silly code since we made it up." She stopped pacing and sat on the edge of the bed. "Damien was acting pretty spaced out. Do you think he was on something? Was he trying to pull something?"

I just groaned in response, too exhausted to speculate on questions I didn't have answers to. She wasn't listening anyway. I could almost see the investigative wheels turning in her head, and she was mostly just talking out loud as she processed her own questions. I was spared the next round of unanswerable questions by a loud knock at the door.

June stopped in her tracks, looked up, and headed for the door. I didn't stir from my place in the center of the bed but watched with interest as she squinted through the peephole before swinging the door open. Standing in the hallway were two uniformed police officers.

The taller of the two addressed June. "Good evening ma'am. I'm Officer Devon Rymer, and this is my partner, Stanley Stark. Are you Francesca Egg?"

I bristled at the officer's mispronunciation of my name, which rhymes with ledge, not leg, if you please. I typically am not bothered when people address me as something that pops out of a chicken's behind, but something about this guy already rubbed me the wrong way. He was tall, well-built, with neatly-trimmed dark hair, and looked to be not much older than my son, Ben, but he exuded an attitude of cocky superiority from all the way across the room, making me want to smack the smug right off his face.

His companion, Officer Stark, stood about a head shorter than Rymer. He suffered from year-long allergies if his red, runny eyes and matching nose were any indication. I wouldn't have been surprised if he wiped his nose with his uniform sleeve. He sneezed loudly, and June and I instinctively offered him a simultaneous *Gesundheit*. June grabbed the box of tissues from the nightstand and held it out toward Officer Sneezy.

"I'm June, but Francie is right over there." She pointed in my direction and the two officers shuffled a little further into our room. I was beginning to wonder what these guys were doing here, and why they were asking specifically for me. Did this have something to do with the magic trick gone wrong? If so, wouldn't I be the wronged party here? Come to think of it, shouldn't Angelina and Damien have sent a doctor or a medic or at least some utterly unqualified hotel employee to check up on me? I shivered involuntarily just thinking about my recent close call. Maybe I could milk this episode for more compensations. At this rate, by the end of the weekend, I might own stock in the DeVille properties. Before I could imagine myself stretched out on the penthouse sofa enjoying the view with a fancy drink in my hand, Officer Annoying broke the spell.

"Ms. Egg?"

"Yes, I'm Francesca Egge." I enunciated my last name hoping he would get the hint. "What seems to be the problem, officer? Is this about the magic show? I told Damien, Mr. DeVille, I was fine. I was just shaken up and needed to lie down. I certainly don't need to fill out a police report. Accidents happen in theater, but the show must go on." Again I asked myself why the police rather than some hotel staff was following up on the incident.

The second officer, Stark was it?, took over the questioning as he inched his way closer to me. "Does this scarf belong to you, Ms. Egge?" He held out the scarf that June had been wearing earlier. It was inside a plastic bag marked Evidence.

My mouth took on the characteristics of the Sahara Desert. I swallowed a few times, trying to work up the appropriate ratio of saliva to sand so I could speak if the need arose. I really didn't think I was going to like what was about to happen next. "Yes, it's mine," I rasped. I had no choice, but to accept ownership since all of my stage props had tags sewn into them with my name clearly embroidered to avoid mix-ups behind the curtain during rehearsals and shows.

Officer Rymer stood still as a statue while Stark closed the gap. I did not feel like they were there to either protect or to serve me. My eyes darted around the room, settling in on June's bewildered stare. I tried to use my mind powers, such as they were, to connect with her thoughts and help me figure out what I was supposed to do next. I got nothing. Just then, the two-way radio at Rymer's belt crackled to life. Stark's did the same. Before either of them could reach for the volume knobs on their devices to silence the radio chatter, a clear female voice coming from Rymer's belt filled the dead air. "The family has been notified and would like the body of Roberto DeVille released to the funeral home for preparation. Possible..." Both officers snapped their radios off mid-transmission. I looked again to June who was now standing behind the two cops. Finally, our telepathy powers were in sync because I knew beyond question she was thinking the same thing I was. "Body? DeVille? What has happened? And why on earth are two cops questioning us in our hotel room?"

"What was that about?" I demanded of the officers. I was mad. I felt Officer Rymer owed me that much. I at least had the right to know what all the questions were about. "Did something happen to Bob? Is he..." I couldn't bring myself to finish the sentence, but I felt it in the pit of my stomach. Bob DeVille was dead.

"That will be all for now ladies. We may be back with more questions, so please don't plan to leave the resort." And just like that, they were gone, a deafening silence replacing the space the two officers left behind.

I sank heavily into the arm chair and stared down at my shaking hands. June followed me over and sat in the matching chair, reaching over and taking both my hands in hers. "Listen, Francie." Her voice was soft but steadfast. "I don't know what's going on, but if it's true, and Bob really is dead, we both know you had nothing to do with it. You were too busy trying to keep both halves of your body attached."

"Ugh. Don't remind me. My head is splitting."

"Let's just leave this to the authorities. I'm sure they're questioning everyone at this stage."

"But June, they asked specifically for me. They had my scarf in an evidence bag for crying out loud. We left it up in the DeVille's suite, and I hardly think a little spilled wine is a crime. If it is, we'd both be doing twenty-five to life by now. Where did they get it, and why didn't Angelina just tell them about the wine spill? I don't like this one little bit. I'm calling Hamm and telling him to come get me."

"Francie, calm down. Let's not get Hamm and Jack worried over nothing. At least, not yet. By morning, I'm sure the police will have everything figured out, and we can still enjoy our plans. I think we all deserve this nice long weekend. I know the guys were really looking forward to their golf tournament, and you got me excited about trying my hand at some theater activities. Let's just call it a night and start fresh in the morning."

I gave in to June's voice of reason, and after flipping through some literature I found on the end table and eating a Hershey bar I had stashed in my purse, I was ready to crawl into bed and give forty winks the old college try.

Chapter Eight

I am a tainted wether of the flock,/ Meetest for death: the weakest kind of fruit/ Drops earliest to the ground. ~*The Merchant of Venice*

Iwoke up to an insistent clanking sound reminding me of a metal cup being dragged across iron bars. I bolted upright in my bed and realized that a voicemail message alert on my cellphone was the source of the clanging, not an agitated prisoner in a jail cell. I had slept fitfully, dreaming about maniacal magicians and murderous scarf-wearing convicts. Tentatively, I ran a hand across my midsection just to make sure I was still in one piece. Little by little, my head began to clear, mostly due to the amazing aroma of robust coffee brewing in the fancy, stainless steel coffee maker on the kitchenette counter. Breathing in the promise of caffeine, I reached for the bedside table and collected my phone to listen to the voicemail I had received sometime during the night.

Hamm had called me at five o'clock in the morning, not technically the middle of the night, but still. He wanted to wish me a fun and exciting day and to apologize again for not letting me know ahead of time that he and Jack had left the marina early to beat the storm. I was relieved that they had made it safely to the golf resort, but the feeling was deflated by his goodbye words informing me that he wouldn't have his phone with him during the day, but I could reach him after their dinner around nine. He was going to leave his phone on its charger like I had asked, so if I needed anything, I should call Jack's phone. I was debating whether or not I should dial him up to fill him in about last night when June popped her head around the counter.

"Good morning sleeping beauty. I thought I was going to have to pour this coffee directly down your throat to wake you up." June, bright-eyed and dressed to impress in a cute khaki skirt and V-neck lavender top, handed me a steaming cup of the aromatic coffee. She was tapping her tan topsiders with purple laces on the vinyl floor of the kitchenette. She no doubt had already finished the first pot.

"Thanks. What time did you wake up? I didn't hear a thing."

"Oh, it was early. I didn't check the clock." June bounced down on the edge of the matching queen-sized bed next to mine, vibrating with energy. "I can't wait to get downstairs for breakfast and to hear what's going on. You should take your coffee into the shower with you. We don't have much time to eat before our first session starts."

With a friend like June, my pensive mood didn't stand a chance. Giving in to her enthusiasm, I decided to leave last night behind me and headed for the shower.

SINCE WE WERE SHORT on time, as June kept reminding me, we filled two plates apiece as we navigated our way through the buffet line. Sitting across the table from June, I couldn't help but grin. There was enough food in front of her to feed three people her size (or two of mine).

"I don't know why this place is called Devil's Island. As far as I'm concerned, it's a little slice of Heaven." June was talking around mouthfuls of cheese-and-spinach quiche, cheese crepes, and cherry cheese danishes. I had to agree that the food was heavenly, and aside from nearly being sawed in half and questioned by the police, the accommodations and service had all been impeccable.

Today was the first day of classes, and in spite of the early hour, the dining hall was full. Conversations were buzzing all around us, and underneath the current of shop talk and arguments over logistics, hushed whispers wafted to the surface.

"...man found dead right here in the resort...authorities not offering much information... messages hand-delivered to guest rooms...possible homicide on the property...all seminars still being held on schedule...resort on lockdown...no one permitted to enter or leave the property until permission was granted by the head detective." We were officially prisoners in paradise.

"How *do* you think the police got ahold of your scarf last night?"

"Hmm?" Just as I was beginning to get into the spirit of things, I was startled out of my musings by June's question. Now she was the one bringing up the topic.

I didn't have time to give the question more consideration because Angelina pulled up a chair and sat down beside me. Dressed entirely in black this morning, her tastefully understated pantsuit draped her curves but managed to look appropriately somber nonetheless. Her wardrobe choice confirmed my dark suspicion that Bob was indeed dead.

"I'm glad you ladies are up and about this morning. After last night, I was worried you might decide to lay low and stay in your room. Your room is suitable, isn't it? If there's anything you need, please call the number on your all-access pass and it will be taken care of right away. Damien feels horrible about the magic trick and sends his apologies. And then there is this tragedy with Bob. Our family is still reeling, trying to sort things out. Managing this resort is all-consuming as you can imagine, and now this. Excuse me. I shouldn't be rambling on about personal problems. How is your breakfast?"

"Everything is fine. Please don't give us a second thought." I poked a strawberry with my fork as I took in the finer details of Angelina's appearance. The delicate skin under her eyes had the slightest tinge of purple, and both her thumbnails showed evidence of having been chewed.

"My most sincere condolences to you and your family." Clearing my throat, I added, "Angelina, I hate to bring this up, but do you have any idea how the police got the scarf that we left in your suite last night? They came to our room last night and had it sealed in an evidence bag. Is there anything we should know about?"

June joined the conversation, having finally swallowed the mouthful of bacon she was chewing on when Angelina arrived. "Bob was never our favorite harbormaster, as you know, but we would never want to see him hurt. I can't imagine this place without him. Do the police have any idea about what happened yet?"

Angelina waved her pale hand as if trying to make the unpleasant topic disappear. "They are following up on some leads." Her voice trailed off, and before the ensuing silence had the chance to become awkward, Angelina's head snapped up in the direction of the silky male voice coming from the illegally handsome man who had appeared out of nowhere. "And who wants to know?"

"Gabriel. You startled me." Angelina stood up and exchanged a quick familial kiss on the cheek with the mystery man. "Please meet Francie and June. They are attending your weekend conference and have become special guests of mine and Damien's. We met them specifically because of some trouble that was stirred up by Bob down at the marina yesterday." She stopped short, probably thinking it was better not to tempt fate.

"Enchanted, ladies. Gabriel DeVille. Any friends of my brother and his lovely wife are certainly friends of mine. Did I notice your names on the registry for my set design seminar this morning? I hope to become better acquainted with you both."

The way his gaze bore into my brain, I felt like the room and all its inhabitants had magically melted away. Gabriel DeVille, although several years younger, was cut from the same cloth as his brother, but where Damien had jet black hair and piercing brown eyes, Gabriel's hair was a light brown, perfectly styled and kissed by the sun. It was impossible to tell whether the highlights were courtesy of Mother Nature or Lady Clairol. His eyes were the clear blue-green of the Caribbean Sea. Same chiseled features, same tall, strong build. Aahh. I mentally slapped my married face and looked over to my single friend who was doing a little melting of her own.

"Before I get finished setting up, Angelina, I was wondering if we could have a quick word?"

Angelina accepted Gabriel's arm, "I'm sure I'll be seeing you ladies later. Do try to enjoy your day. "

"Holy Adonis." June was licking her lips like a cat in a cream bowl as she gazed in admiration at the suave Gabriel ushering Angelina away on the crook of his elbow. "I hate to speak ill of the dead, but those DeVille men are gorgeous. Except Bob. He may have fallen out of the ugly tree and hit every branch on the way down. Don't you think?"

"I certainly won't mind spending the next few hours staring at Gabriel DeVille as he presents the set design lecture. As for Bob, I think his outward appearance was a reflection of his dejected, hateful, poor me..."

Someone was tapping my shoulder. By the look on June's face, I assumed it was not someone who needed to hear my inappropriate slandering of the recently-departed Bob. I turned slowly in my chair to face officers Rymer and Stark. "Uh, good morning officers." I put on the best variation of my sweet and innocent face I could muster up in a split-second.

"Ms. Egge, this is Detective Evelyn Reed. She is going to be conducting the investigation of Mr. DeVille's homicide. You will want to cooperate fully, I'm sure." Officer Stark moved aside, allowing the detective, the latest in the ever-expanding lineup of people I didn't care to meet, to step forward. She was pretty, but not in a flashy way. Her strawberry blond hair was pulled back in a low ponytail, and minimal makeup allowed a light sprinkle of freckles to decorate her nose and cheeks. It also allowed the dark circles below her eyes to betray the evidence of a sleepless night.

"Wait a minute. You're saying Bob was murdered?" Stark's remark added the gruesome fact that his death was not accidental. Was my scarf somehow used in a crime? I was heading down that dark path of doubt once more.

Detective Reed's gaze scanned our breakfast spread and methodically took in every inch of our space, cataloguing each minute detail before coming to rest on the lavender and rose designer scarf June had looped around her neck just before leaving our room. I hadn't even considered the implication of her adorning her casual outfit with a jaunty scarf that morning until Detective Reed honed in on it. "Good morning ladies. I just wanted to introduce myself and inform you that I will need to ask both of you some questions later today. I assume you will be here in the hotel for the remainder of the morning?"

As unruffled as always, June recited our entire schedule for the day and then stood up from the table ready to head to the fifth floor for our first workshop. "We'll talk to you later, Detective. I don't want to be late. Come on Francie."

Chapter Nine

Love looks not with the eyes, but with the mind, and
therefore is winged cupid painted blind.
~A Midsummer Night's Dream

After taking our seats at one of the long tables in the
fifth-floor conference room, I felt like I could finally relax
again. "How do you do it June? You just blew that detective off
and acted like you weren't even concerned that we are going to
be questioned for the second time in connection to a murder."

"Well, we didn't do it, did we?"

"No, but still, I think we're under suspicion."

"If we didn't do anything wrong, then they can't prove that
we did, so what's the sense of getting all worked up?"

"I guess you're right. Somehow I always end up feeling
guilty even when I have nothing to hide. I suppose we should
just try to enjoy ourselves and let the investigators find out who
the real killer is. Do you think the person is still here on the
island?"

June didn't have a chance to answer. A short man resembling a ferret in a dreadful Hawaiian shirt barreled into the room. I held my breath waiting for the sleeping rodent on top of his head to spring to life and bite me, but thankfully the faux hair stayed put, and I was not subjected to whatever hid beneath it. I mean, really, as bad as that thing looked, I had no desire to find out the true condition of his scalp. Weasel guy pulled a chair from the end of the long conference table and dragged it until he managed to maneuver himself into the space right between June and me. We were the only three people in the room and were now crowded together like the proverbial sardines in a tin.

"Hi. I'm Eddie. Eddie Sneed. You're Francie and June right?" His beady black eyes darted left to right and right to left, never coming to rest on either one of us, which may have been a good thing. "Are you the ones who killed that guy in the stairwell? I heard all about you. You caught that killer on Kelleys Island right? Are you undercover agents? Man, I can't believe I got into this lecture with you. Everyone was all hyped up about that theater makeup demonstration, but when I saw the two of you signed up for this session, I just had to sign up. If we do a group activity can I be in your group? Can I help you catch the killer? What are you doing for lunch? I'm free, if you are planning to do some sleuthing. I'm really good at blending in."

"Gooood morning set designers." Gabriel swooped into the room with a robust greeting obviously meant for more than three attendees. He missed half a beat in his introduction as he scanned the conference area looking for the rest of the participants, but all he found was two ladies and a weasel-faced man scrunched shoulder-to-shoulder at the center table surrounded by at least thirty empty chairs. At least Eddie Sneed finally shut his pie hole when Gabriel entered.

"Well, this is a bit more intimate than I had foreseen." Gabriel pulled up a chair and sat on the opposite side of the table facing us. "I'm not entirely surprised though. I guess word got out about the theater makeup demonstration. It's supposed to be pretty entertaining this year."

June leaned halfway across the table toward Gabriel. "I don't see how we could complain about getting your undivided personal attention. It's their loss, right guys?" She was addressing us, but never took her eyes off our instructor.

Gabriel held June's gaze, and I started to feel like I was intruding on an intimate moment, until I heard the ding of an incoming text message from the pocket of her tan skirt. She reached discreetly under the table to retrieve her phone and sneak a peek at the screen. The spell was broken, and June's cheeks were now blooming sweetheart-rose red. I couldn't see around Eddie at what she was looking at, and he was stretching his neck over her shoulder obviously trying to get a look himself. I would just have to wait until we were alone to ask her about it, but I had a suspicion that Jack Morgan had something to do with her high color. Geesh, she was going to need to whip out her notebook soon to keep track of all the handsome men she was flirting with. Between the dreamy detective from Kelleys Island, and the rich, handsome business mogul, she had better be careful. I felt no jealousy toward my friend, though. My hubby was all I needed or wanted, even after more than twenty years of marriage, and it didn't hurt that he was still in great shape and looked a lot like George Clooney.

"So what are we going to do today? Are we building a set? Is there going to be time to get a snack? Do we need a pen and paper? Is there going to be a group project?" Eddie Sneed was starting to remind me of a naughty puppy that needed a swift dose of discipline.

Gabriel cleared his throat obviously trying to conceal a groan. June reflexively slapped her hand over Eddie's mouth to shut him up, and I lowered my forehead to the cherrywood table seriously considering banging it a few times. And that is when Detective Reed walked into the room.

"Excuse me, I hope I'm not interrupting something too important. Are you acting out some sort of scene?" She stepped into the room and closed the door behind her. "I can wait a minute if you want to finish up. This looks interesting."

Gabriel regained his composure first. "Hello again, Detective. We were actually just getting acquainted. What can we do for you?"

"I need to speak with Francesca and June, separately, for a few minutes, if you can spare them."

"Of course. Anything we can do to help out." My non-guilty, guilty conscience was rearing its ugly head again as Gabriel offered me up to the detective like a sacrificial lamb.

"Ms. Egge, shall we go into the hall to speak?"

I didn't feel like I had a choice, so I got up and followed her into the empty hallway. As the detective pulled the door closed behind us, I could hear Eddie start in on another round of rapid-fire questions. I was almost relieved to be leaving the room. Almost.

Reed stood with her back to the door and her arms crossed over her chest presenting an intimidating figure despite her petite proportions. I was left trying to figure out what to do with my hands and whether or not I should make eye contact.

"Francie, may I call you Francie? I need to ask you a few questions."

"Yes, of course, that's fine, but I don't have any idea what I could possibly contribute to your investigation."

" Where were you during the storm and power outage?"

Nothing like getting right to the point, I thought. I took a deep breath and began relaying the details of yesterday evening. "I was with June. We got caught in the rain between the marina and the hotel. The power went out just before we entered the lobby, so we took the stairs. Something was blocking the door to the stairwell." As I retold the story, I realized that the "something" was not an oversized laundry bag, but Bob's makeshift body bag. I shuddered involuntarily as I remembered the sound it made as it thumped over onto the floor in front of us and how we unceremoniously stepped over it in a hurry to get upstairs.

"Thank you. Now, can you tell me about your scarf?"

"My scarf? What does my scarf have to do with any of this?"

"If you don't mind, Francie, I'll ask the questions. Where did you get the scarf?"

"I got it last year at a drama seminar. There are always small props and costume elements that are given out or sold at discounted prices as incentives from various suppliers. I thought it was pretty and I bought it, simple as that. As a courtesy, the suppliers engrave or embroider the purchaser's name on the item and keep it till check-out. That way, nothing gets lost or mixed up."

"To your knowledge, does anyone else own a scarf like that one?"

"How should I know?" I heard the high-pitched tone of my own voice, and made a mental note to calm down so Reed would not equate my irritation and frustration with her questions to guilt of some kind.

She ignored my reaction and moved on to her next question. "When did you notice your scarf was missing? Do you have any idea where you lost it?"

"What? It was never missing. I didn't lose it. Didn't Angelina tell you?"

The detective tilted her head and stared at me. "What would Mrs. DeVille have to tell me about your scarf?"

I calmly explained to her about the wine spill in the DeVille's penthouse and how Angelina insisted on having it laundered.

Reed referred to the notepad she was holding and jotted a few notes I couldn't see. She questioned me about who, if anyone, had seen us during the time we were caught in the storm.

"I don't remember seeing anyone at all while we were out in the rain or when we came back. Let's face it, no one wanted to be out in that weather, least of all me."

"Thank you, Francie. That's all I need for now. You can go back to your session. You've been most helpful."

"Okay, but I still don't see how any of this can be at all useful."

The detective kept her gaze fixed on her notebook. "Please send June out if you would be so kind."

I reluctantly re-entered the conference room, slumped into the chair at the end of the table, and relayed Reed's invitation to June. She had been chatting amiably with Gabriel while doing her best to ignore Eddie without being too obvious. She stood reluctantly and headed out into the hall, closing the door behind her.

Chapter Ten

But I will wear my heart upon my sleeve/For daws to peck at. I am not what I am. ~*Othello*

The mood had definitely been altered by the visit from Detective Reed. We were all back in the conference room, but the seating arrangement had been purposefully altered. When June returned from her hallway interrogation, she made sure there was an empty chair between me, my friend, and our annoying classmate. Eddie started to speak but must have seen the death rays shooting toward his brain from both directions and thought better of it. Gabriel had been pacing in the front of the room, hands deep in his pockets, eyes dark and brooding. After a minute, he approached our table, gathered up some papers, tapping their edges into a neat pile and sat back down across from us. He seemed to understand that we were not really in the right mindset to listen to a technical rendering of the ins and outs of theater set design. After putting his notes away in his briefcase, he inhaled thoughtfully and spoke.

"I have a proposition for the three of you. I am in charge of the final night event. It's a mystery dinner theater featuring attendees of this conference who have signed up to participate and showcase some of their special skills. Why don't we wrap up early in here and then meet later, perhaps after the afternoon lecture, in the main theater. The final night dinner theater will be in the Crystal Theater where you were last night, but it will be in use this evening, so we can meet in the original Starlight Theater. We don't use it very often anymore, but it's a real treasure. I'm sure you'll enjoy a private tour of the facility. Then you can help me orchestrate the line-up, and we can discuss set design in a more hands-on environment. I should have the full list of participants by then."

I blew out a sigh of relief. I didn't think I could sit here and concentrate much longer because I really wanted to hear what Detective Reed had asked June and compare stories. "I think that sounds great. What do you guys think?" I included Eddie in my question even though I was speaking directly to June. "Let's make it four o'clock then, after the lecture. I have no problem missing the meet and greet with the cast of tonight's mini-performance."

"Sounds delightful to me." June was once again staring dreamily at Gabriel, no doubt glad for another opportunity to spend some quality time with him.

Without waiting for Eddie to add his opinion of the plan or to launch into his newest round of questions, we grabbed our purses and headed for the door. Unfortunately, he didn't get the hint. Eddie popped out of his chair and followed close on our heels, resuming his relentless queries about our lunch and investigating plans. When I looked back into the room searching for an excuse to leave our new-found parasite behind, I saw that Gabriel was deep in conversation on his cell phone. His voice was hushed and his forehead was creased. He looked at his watch then stormed out through a door on the opposite side of the room. No longer did he appear the least bit concerned about the low attendance of his session or the caliber of his students.

We got off the elevator on the twelfth floor and had to physically stop Eddie from following us out. We promised to meet him at the trade show where lunch was also being served. Once safely inside our room behind the locked door, June and I started shooting rapid-fire words over one another, sounding more like Eddie than either of us would care to admit.

"Hang on Francie. Let's take this one step at a time. I need to get a feel for this situation from the beginning. You go first. What did Detective Reed ask you?"

"Okay, let's see. She wanted to know where we were during the storm and power outage. Then she asked a bunch of questions about that stupid scarf. She wanted to know where I got it, if anyone else had one like it that I knew of, and when exactly I lost it. I told her that it wasn't lost. I explained about the wine in the DeVille's penthouse and how we left it there because Angelina insisted on having it laundered. She was adamant to know if anyone had seen us during the time we were caught in the storm. I don't remember seeing anyone at all while we were out in the rain or when we came back. I don't think we have an alibi, June. Someone must have killed Bob when the power was out and left him in that stairwell, and we have no proof that it wasn't us. Add our little scene with Bob earlier in the day and whatever that scarf has to do with things, and it doesn't look good. I think I should call Hamm. I might need a lawyer."

"Not yet, Francie. I don't think you need to worry Hammond. As far as I know, they've still got this whole place closed off, and he couldn't come anyway. Besides, I really don't want Jack to think we can't be left unattended for a single weekend without getting ourselves sucked into a murder investigation."

"Okay, I guess you're right. We're not in danger, and the cops must be following up on some other clues besides the ones that involve us. So, what did Reed ask you about?"

"She asked me the same things mostly. I told her that I was the one wearing your scarf and that I was the one who pushed Bob into the lake. The one thing that does bother me about this investigation is that she really seemed to be focusing on you for some reason. It almost looks as if you're being set up. Why wouldn't Angelina just tell the police about what happened in the suite? What could she possibly have to hide?"

"I have no idea why someone would want to accuse me of murder, and the more I think about it, the more I am sure that we need to get to the bottom of this before I find myself in a very serious situation."

June was uncharacteristically pensive for the next few minutes. Then like a light switch being flipped on, she went into investigator mode. "Here's what we'll do..."

A soft knock on the door interrupted June's synopsis of her plan. She hopped over to the door and swung it open with enough force to make the girl in the hallway squeal like a cat whose tail had been slammed by the pantry door. "What now?" June was at the end of her patience.

"Um, I have the spa passes you requested." I could hear the young girl's accent even though she barely spoke above a whisper. She couldn't have been more than nineteen years old and looked to be of European descent just like so many of the seasonal employees on Lake Erie.

"We didn't request any spa services. Who are they from?" June grabbed the passes from the girl's hand and scanned the small print to see if she could discover who had sent the service tickets. The girl began to retreat from the doorway, back toward the elevators. "Hang on a minute." June's curt command stopped the girl in her tracks. "Aren't you that girl who was in the DeVille's suite last night? What's your name?"

"My name is Sasha." Between the girl's accent and the tentative whisper of her voice, I could barely make out what she was saying. "I really need to get back to work. If there was a mix-up with your spa order you can contact the concierge and I'm sure he can straighten it out. I'm so sorry to interrupt you."

June wasn't satisfied with this information. "Not so fast. Come into the room for a minute so I can call the front desk. I'm sure you'll just have to come back in a few minutes to pick these back up, anyway. I'm sorry I yelled at you. It's not your fault. Please come in."

Sasha hesitated for a split-second, then turned and bolted down the hall to the stairs and disappeared.

Chapter Eleven

There is nothing either good or bad, but thinking makes it so.
~Hamlet

Murder investigation aside, I was looking forward to a nice lunch chatting with the actors who would be performing in the mini-production of *Much Ado About Nothing* at seven o'clock. Was it too much to ask for one hour void of drama or intrigue except for what was happening on stage? I was also hoping to run into Angelina or Damien again. I wanted some answers as to why Angelina was continuing to let the police believe that my scarf had been lost somewhere rather than being left in her care at her own insistence.

As June and I made our way over to the Great Hall shortly after noon, I noticed a disquieting theme among the people in our vicinity. "June, am I seeing things or are there zombies about?"

"Huh?" June looked up from her cell phone where she had been posting or tweeting or texting or something.

"Earth to June. Could you please return to the moment and help me figure out why there are zombies milling about. I expected to see Leonato, Hero, Beatrice, and Margaret, not the cast from The Walking Dead."

When a shuffling, rotting, corpse-like figure bumped into June and wordlessly moved on, she finally reacted. "Hey, Aaa..., I mean, Jerk! Watch where you're going!" (She should talk.) She finally focused on our surroundings, turning in a complete circle in the middle of the hall.

"Hey Francie, what's up with the zombies? I thought you said we were lunching with Shakespearean characters. It's been a long time since I've read anything by old William, but as far as I can recall, there weren't any references to the undead in his plays. Zombies are much cooler though. I wonder if I could get one of them to talk to me."

"They're coming out of the elevator and heading for the Great Hall. I wonder if they're on the hunt for sandwiches or ladyfingers." My initial shock at seeing the place overrun with the ghoulish creatures, gave way to a professional appreciation for what was happening. "I remember now. The theatrical make-up session was up on the third floor at the same time our session was scheduled. Wow! They really went all out. Kind of makes me wish we had picked that class instead of ending up being harangued by Eddie Sneed and questioned by the detective."

"True, but at least we got to meet Gabriel DeVille. Did you see how he kept looking at me? He even complimented me on my fashion sense." She twirled the end of her borrowed scarf around her finger absentmindedly. "I told you not to get so worked up about me wearing this scarf today. It's not like I'm wearing a smoking gun around my neck."

"Yes, June, I saw. Not to take away from the power of your charms, dear, but he had pretty limited options, wouldn't you agree?"

"Spoilsport!"

"Just don't spill anything on this scarf or leave it behind anywhere. I'd hate to have another accessory taken into police custody, unless, of course, it's the fashion police."

"Hmmph."

"How soon you forget. Jack Morgan hasn't been out of your sight more than a day, and you're already mooning over a guy you don't even know."

"Hey, we're not engaged, so what's the harm in a little flirting?"

"Suit yourself. I just think you ought to think things through for once. Oh, the heck with it. Let's go get something to eat."

Standing in the buffet line gave us an opportunity to get the full effect of the results of the theatrical makeup class. In addition to the zombies, there were apparent victims of various types of violence—gunshot wounds, stabbings, burns, and all sorts of non-appetizing special effects. Maybe I would write a suggestion for the organizers to rethink the timing of this particular workshop. Then again, maybe they did it on purpose hoping people might have smaller appetites when they came down for lunch.

June elbowed me in the ribs. "Ouch! What's the deal!"

"Look over there, next to the beverage table. Isn't that Sasha, the girl with the spa tickets?"

"Stop pointing, June, it's rude. But yes, it sure is." Sasha, the Russian jill-of-all-trades, was standing against the wall looking terrified. Or maybe it was sheer exhaustion. She seemed to be turning up everywhere we went, and so far, she never appeared relaxed or happy. "She must be working non-stop over the summer to pay for college. I wonder if she's thinking about going into show business or special effects makeup. That black eye looks very convincing."

We made our way across the room, being careful not to tip our trays or collide with any of the shuffling, swaying bodies who seemed to be multiplying by the second. Knowing that they were fellow seminar participants did little to deflect the overall effect their appearance inspired. I was torn between asking for the name of the makeup artist for future reference and avoiding them like the plague. Did I just say that? Oh well, I really didn't want to get up close or personal with the milling monsters. Finally, we settled on a round table and claimed two of its six vacant chairs. Eating a meal surrounded by zombies was more interesting than it was frightening, but when a trio of clowns in full costume and makeup pulled up seats at our table, I nearly choked on my potato salad.

I diverted my eyes and concentrated on my watch. "Would you look at the time? We better get going, June. We don't want to be late for our next session."

June got it. She isn't a big fan of sinister circus entertainers either, so she left her uneaten mashed potatoes and macaroni and cheese and followed my lead. The clowns remained still and silent. They didn't even have lunch trays. I couldn't tell if it was the makeup or if they were really leering at us, but I wasn't about to stick around to find out.

Chapter Twelve

Though this be madness, yet there is method in 't. *~Hamlet*

The afternoon was progressing nicely. We were seated near the back of the Armstrong Lecture Hall attending a special lecture—Puppetry: Bringing Life to Marionettes. It was proving to be very informative, if not a little creepy, after our lunchtime encounter with the zombies and clowns. Puppets were about halfway down on my list of freaks, so after about an hour and a half, I felt a bit antsy and started daydreaming. Plus, my butt was getting numb.

I fumbled in my handbag and located my cell phone. Pressing the wake-up button, I saw 3:45 displayed on my home screen and decided we had officially learned everything we needed to know about marionettes. "June," I whispered, "let's bug out now before the lecture ends. I need to stretch my legs, and we can stop at the bar for a glass of wine before we meet Gabriel in the theater. What do you say?"

"I say let's do it. I can't believe we've been sitting in these uncomfortable seats for as long as we have. Who knew puppets could be so fascinating?" I wasn't sure if she was being serious or sarcastic, but I didn't really care. She was out of her seat and down the aisle ahead of me.

When we got to the lobby, the lounge was deserted except for the bored looking man polishing glasses behind the bar. None of the conference workshops had officially let out yet, and the other hotel guests were most likely clinging to safety bars and screaming on the thrill rides in the amusement park or wending their way down the Lazy River in the water park. No one was giving up the glorious afternoon sunshine in favor of a dimly lit bar. It was perfect. We pulled out two bar stools, made ourselves comfortable, and placed our order.

"Now this is the life. An afternoon cocktail with my best friend and no questions or disconcerting stares from inquisitive strangers or investigators."

"Cheers to that, Francie!"

We clinked our glasses and savored the first cool sip of our wine. As I set my glass down on the bar, I noticed Angelina walking past the lounge. I raised my hand and tried to make eye contact, but she quickened her pace and became suddenly very preoccupied with the phone in her hand.

"Did you see that June? I think Angelina is trying to avoid us. What do you think she's up to?"

"Maybe she's just busy. I'm sure it takes a lot to run this resort, and with the added stress of trying to appease all the people who aren't allowed to leave the hotel, plus a funeral to plan, I'm sure we're the least of her worries."

"You're right of course, but something just feels off."

Fortified with a few handfuls of mixed nuts and a glass of chardonnay, we hopped off our bar stools and made our way over to the theater for our meeting with Gabriel. June was a bit over-anxious considering we were going to plan the logistics of a mystery dinner theater put on by virtual strangers. She swung open the doors, ready with the bright smile and self-confident swagger that she managed to make look cute and sexy at the same time. "Hello!" Her greeting echoed back to us in the cavernous space. Other than the stage lights, the huge old theater was dark. The place looked deserted. I stood for a moment inhaling deeply the essence of my college years, remembering all the possibilities of the empty stage.

June, deflated now, stood beside me still as a stone. Her voice was soft and tentative now. "He did say four o'clock in the theater, didn't he, Francie?"

"It's only five after four. He's probably just running a little late. Let's see if we can find the light switch." I made my way around the perimeter of the dimly-lit room, locating a bank of switches near the emergency exit door. Click, click, click. Bright light flooded the space, illuminating the rich burgundy velvet of the theater seats. I've been in a lot of theaters, and this one was definitely up there in the top three for opulence, comfort, and cleanliness. It was hard to believe the Starlight Theater was no longer used on a regular basis.

Now that the lights were on, I spotted a note written on a sheet of creamy embossed stationery taped to the wall beside the entrance door. I could see the gilded letter D at the top of the paper from across the room, a clear indication of the author's identity. Retracing my steps, I retrieved the note and read it out loud.

"Had to go to the prop room to grab some supplies. Be back in a flash. Make yourselves comfortable. —G.D."

"See, just like I said. He'll be here in a few minutes. Let's just…What the heck? Did you turn the lights back out?"

"Sshh. Do you hear that Francie?"

I stood still and listened in the dark; the soft swishing sound was coming from behind and above us. I turned just in time to see a bright beam of light coming from the old-fashioned projection booth and spotlighting a screen up on stage that I didn't notice until right now.

June and I sat down uneasily in the last row of seats and stared straight ahead. I had a bad feeling about this.

Scratchy black-and-white images appeared silently on the screen. After about five seconds of indecipherable film, a series of distinct pictures emerged. It looked like one of those news clips where people tell their stories by holding up a series of placards, only this wasn't about a courageous teenager, a mother's love, or a patient who beat the odds. In fact, there was nothing uplifting whatsoever in the message.

The first clip was an ominous-looking clown dressed all in black. He wore a black wig, and a leering black smile slashed his chalk-white face nearly in two. He held three posters in front of him. After about a three-second zoom on the first one proclaiming, *You Knew Bob*, he tossed it on the floor, and the camera held steady on his second message, *Bob Knew Us*. His final poster read, *We Know You*. Next, the film transitioned in a fade-out to a second video clip. It was another clown, but this one was dressed in white from head to toe. He wore a tall, pointy hat with a big pom-pom at the tip. His blood-red smile had no mirth in it. In his white-gloved hands was his own series of poster messages which he held and tossed in the same manner as clown number one: *If You're Smart/Learn the Plan/*

And Follow Through. By the time the third escapee from camp creepy appeared, we were holding each other's hands so tightly my fingers were numb. I stared at the ghoulish figure praying that his performance was the last part of the message. This clown, decked out in crimson, had a devilish quality about him. He wore a close-fitting hood that met his neck in a bouncy flounce of red ruffles. His skin was painted a perfect match to his costume, but, unlike the other two, there were no exaggerated facial features added to his countenance. Truth be told, his eyes looked a little scared. The messages he held in front of him at arm's length were scrawled in white paint on black posters: *Get The Proof/Pack Your Bags/Seal Your Fate.*

The screen melted back into gray snow and then the light from the projector went out, and we were plunged into inky darkness for the second time. My nerves were jangling, my hands were shaking, and my teeth were chattering. Finally, I screamed. June's own wail of distress matched mine octave for octave.

Could this get any worse? Oh yes it could. A real-life clown in full regalia wielding a flashlight, peeked out from behind the curtain, then ran across the stage and out the exit on the opposite side. Really? Had one of our earlier lunch mates followed us to the theater? It wasn't like we needed to pick up our sparkling conversation. Was he trying to find his two buddies, or just making sure we had received the intended special feature? Before I could give it more thought, I nearly rocketed out of my seat when I heard a velvety voice ask, "What's going on in here? Why are you two sitting in the dark? And where is Mr. Sneed?"

Chapter Thirteen

I am very proud, revengeful, ambitious, with more offences at my beck than I have thoughts to put them in,/ Imagination to give them shape, or time to act them in. *~Hamlet*

I had completely forgotten that Eddie was part of our class and by rights should have been with us in the theater. He had been so anxious to join us. We hadn't run into him at lunch, but with all the other interesting characters in the Great Hall, his absence never even registered with me. Now though, it did seem odd that he was nowhere to be found.

Gabriel flicked the light switch, and the theater was once again illuminated as if nothing strange had happened. However, here in the light, I could tell that June's hands were shaking as much as mine, and beads of perspiration stood out on her forehead. Although I couldn't see it, I was pretty sure her heart was racing in her chest. Mine was.

June was able to regain her composure before I was, so she recapped the entire incident for Gabriel from our arrival at the theater, to the terrifying video messages, to the appearance of the flesh-and-blood mystery clown.

"You're going to want to look at the video, Gabriel. It's very disturbing. I don't know who this was intended for, but either I'm being paranoid, or this message was actually meant for Francie and me. Who would want to do such a horrible thing, and why? It doesn't make sense. We don't know anything about Bob's personal life, nor do we care about it. I'd like to know who is trying to pull us into this whole sorry mess." June stopped her monologue and looked at Gabriel. "Oh, I'm sorry. I guess that remark was insensitive."

"There's no need for you to apologize, June. It sounds like you're the victim here. And as for my brother, it wouldn't be the first time his presence disturbed someone."

I thought Gabriel's assessment was fair; however, although true, it seemed a little cold-hearted under the circumstances. But then again, people dealt with grief in many different ways.

"Let's calm down and think this through," Gabriel suggested. "My recommendation is that we call the police and give them the video. I'll go up and get it and keep it in the safe in my office until we can turn it over. They can dust the projection booth for fingerprints and look for other clues. Did you see anyone besides the mystery clown in the theater, anyone at all?"

"How could we?" I answered. "It was pitch dark when we first got here."

"The creepy clown didn't stick around to chat," June added.

Gabriel had gone silent, so when he spoke next, I wasn't expecting it. "Oh, I'll get to the bottom of this, don't you worry, ladies."

My feelings echoed his. Tucking my fear away, I made up my mind to be proactive. "I'm not going to stand around and let some demented clowns terrorize us. If this is supposed to be a joke, I'm not at all amused. I'm going upstairs to that projection booth myself and see if I can find out what's going on. Are you coming, June?"

I didn't have to ask. She was already heading for the door in the lobby marked Projection Booth—Authorized Personnel Only. Her expression was impossible to misconstrue. "Stay out of my way and don't mess with me."

The small room looked perfectly innocuous. There were three large old-fashioned reel-to-reel projectors mounted to the floor, each pointed at its own square window to the stage and screen. Set apart a short distance, at the end of the row, was a single digital projector. All three of the old-fashioned projectors were still warm, but there wasn't a film strip to be found among them. What did we expect, a signed note? I headed over to the modern machine and examined it. More nothing.

"Hey wait. What's this?" I bent down and stretched my arm to the back side of the projector, near the wall, to retrieve the red object.

June stared at the small rubber sphere in my outstretched hand. "Looks like a clown nose to me. Yep, definitely a clown nose. Did you notice whether or not that jogging jester was missing any clown-type body parts?"

Now that I had spoiled the one piece of potentially helpful evidence, I felt a little embarrassed. We were no closer to figuring out who was behind the incident, and now it seemed like calling the police would only draw unwanted attention to ourselves. And to top it off, Eddie Sneed was still AWOL.

"It's unfortunate, I know, but I see no reason to do any mystery dinner theater planning or set designing now. I apologize for the inconvenience and am more than happy to refund you both the price of the seminar. When I find out Mr. Sneed's circumstances, I will deal with him accordingly." There was an undercurrent of suppressed anger in his voice. "Dinner is scheduled from five until six thirty. It's already close to five, so you might as well head out. Please enjoy your dinner and don't worry too much about what just happened. I'll get to the bottom of it." With that, Gabriel left us.

"Let's get out of here," I said. "I've had just about enough of all of this. I could use a drink. Or two."

"I'm right there with you." June pulled the door shut behind us, and we made our way back through the hotel and out into the warm evening. A fresh breeze made everything feel clean and ordinary, that is, until I thought about the fact that someone was either trying to get us to do something shady, or worse, frame us for Bob's murder.

Chapter Fourteen

Do you think because you are virtuous, that there shall be no more cakes and ale? ~ *Twelfth Night*

As we walked the short distance from the hotel complex to the amusement park entrance, the topics of murder and malicious clowns prevented me from fully appreciating our surroundings. The smell of popcorn and cotton candy from the vendors stationed on every corner tantalized my olfactory nerves and tickled my taste buds, and there were plenty of interesting people doing plenty of interesting things to keep our minds occupied until we reached the Sky Chair, the ride that reminded me of a ski lift and traversed the entire length of the park. Even with plenty of stimulation for all five senses, it was my sixth sense that was currently occupying all my attention. My need for self-preservation kept getting in the way of enjoying my present environment.

"June, what are we going to do about those clowns? Who are they and how did Bob know them? Do you think they work somewhere in the resort?"

June was chewing on her lower lip. "That's as good a guess as any. Why do they think we can 'learn the plan,' and ditch the proof?' What proof? and what are we supposed to do with it?"

"That's exactly what I'd like to know. Do you think we should tell Detective Reed? Maybe she can track down the clown from the theater. I'm sure he has something to do with this. He must have taken the film with him, even if he's not the one responsible for making it."

"I'm pretty sure Gabriel will share the details with the authorities. His brother was a big part of the message in the video, and they'll want to figure out if it has anything to do with Bob's murder. No doubt Reed and the gang will be back to question us again, probably in the middle of our next session."

"Is it just me, or did Gabriel seem more upset about Eddie Sneed being absent than us being targeted by demented clowns? My head is spinning like the Tilt-a-Whirl."

June didn't answer me. I guessed it was because she had a soft spot for Gabriel.

"What if Eddie was the mystery clown?" I ventured.

"I don't know. I think he was taller than Sneed. Plus, Eddie probably wouldn't have been able to resist stopping to chat. We're almost at the Sky Chair. One thing we can figure out right now is where we should eat dinner."

"How about The Cheesecake Factory? Their food is good, they serve drinks, and of course there's the cheesecake." June didn't offer a single objection to my suggestion.

The main dining and pub section of the park was two blocks long. The restaurants ranged widely in price and scope from dogs and fries to miso salmon and mushroom risotto. The Cheesecake Factory was a new addition to the strip; and therefore, it was located at the end of the street, right where the Sky Chair let us off.

In the last few years, there had been so many additions and improvements to the already amazing island getaway. It must be difficult for the DeVille's to stay ahead of the family entertainment game with all the new and exciting resorts and indoor water parks popping up like weeds and competing for a share of the tourist pie.

We were seated by a cheery hostess in a yellow dress who asked if we would like to see the wine list. "Yes!" times two was what she heard in response to that silly question. We ordered without delay and she scurried off to do our biddings.

We sipped our drinks, and although I was gradually relaxing, I couldn't get rid of the feeling that things were about to get worse. Like it or not, things were happening around us that we had no control over, but would definitely affect us. We still had a lot of thinking to do. But for the time being, I would just concentrate on the menu and what I would order for dinner.

When I had made up my mind, I looked up, intending to ask my friend what she was having, but June was looking over my shoulder in the direction of the kitchen. "This resort is a lot smaller than I thought it was," she said, her eyebrows scrunched together and her lips all bunched up.

"Why would you say that? This place is huge."

"Then why do we keep seeing the same people everywhere we go? I mean, really, how many jobs can that Sasha chick have?"

"What?" I turned my head and shoulders and stretched my neck to follow June's gaze. The restaurant was busy, so it took me a few seconds to zero in on her. There she was, wearing the same sunny dress as our hostess and the rest of the waitresses, so it was clear that she was an employee of the restaurant. At the moment, she was standing in the doorway to the kitchen, her profile silhouetted by the bright lights of the workspace behind her. Her eyes were downcast and her hands were empty, arms straight at her sides. It was obvious that she was being spoken to by an authority figure. Truth be told, she was undeniably being reprimanded or scolded. Or threatened? The person dominating the conversation was just beyond the doorway, out of sight. After about thirty seconds more, Sasha was nudged from the doorway toward the dining room full of seated patrons, and right behind her strode Gabriel DeVille. Gabriel? First we find this girl running from the DeVille penthouse crying, next she shows up at the magic show in the middle of my failed magic act with an unordered cocktail for June, and most recently at our hotel room door with spa passes neither of us ordered. Oh, I almost forgot, she was mingling with the zombies at lunch this afternoon. And now she was heading straight for our table.

"Hello. My name is Sasha and I will be taking care of you this evening. I see you have your drinks. Are you ready to place an order?" She finally finished her scripted greeting and looked up. Her round eyes became even rounder in surprised recognition, and then she promptly dropped her order pad. As she bent down to retrieve it, June gave me a laser-beam stare that went directly into my brain. Neither of us spoke, but I knew exactly what her mind was relaying to mine. "Did you see her face? She has a black eye. A real black eye." My mind acknowledged that I did.

Upright again and composed, she apologized for being clumsy and asked for the second time in her soft accent if we would like to place an order. Suddenly, I wasn't feeling very hungry but didn't want the scene to get any more awkward than it already was, so I quickly scanned the menu and made up my mind.

"I'll have a Caesar salad. June, do you want to split a Godiva chocolate cheesecake?"

"To tell you the truth, I haven't been much in the mood for chocolate since I bought that fancy box at the Memorial Day party and ended up losing a big chunk of time."

I understood completely. June had suffered the dangerous effects of an experimental poison laced into the pretty confections. Though they were intended for someone else, she had suffered the result. The memory was still fresh in both our minds.

"How about strawberry then?" I didn't want to think about those events any more than she did.

"Sure. That sounds good, and I'll have the same salad. And another glass of wine please."

"Make that two," I added.

I was impressed by how Sasha maintained her composure. "Very good, ma'am. I'll put that right in." As soon as she walked away, Gabriel, who had been mingling with the other dinner guests, made a beeline for our table. Oh brother. So far the Drama Divas Convention was sadly living up to its name. I was pretty sure it had been Gabriel berating Sasha just moments ago, but here was June, batting her long eyelashes and running her fingers through her spiky blond hair.

"Good evening ladies! I'm so glad you chose this place for your meal. Do you mind if I join you?"

"Please, sit down," June said without hesitation. More eyelash batting.

The three of us spent the next hour or so eating salad and cheesecake and sipping on some nice pinot noir. I had to try to keep myself occupied and act like I didn't notice while June and Gabriel talked to one another like they were the only two people in the place. One thought that crossed my mind was how did Gabriel get here before us? He must have a private car or taxi or something to zip around in as he surveys his kingdom. Over the course of the meal, as I moved lettuce and croutons around on my plate and swallowed more than my share of the cheesecake, I learned some interesting facts about Gabriel and the DeVille family. The DeVilles, as I had recently discovered, owned the entire Devil's Island Resort, including the five-star hotel and conference center, the restaurants and spa, the amusement park, and the entire marina. I had also recently learned that Damien and his wife, Angelina, managed the hotel and hospitality end of the business. And then there was the recently-departed Roberto, aka Bob, whom we had known for years as the crude and irritating marina manager. What was news to me, was that Gabriel currently lived in Chicago and was an active member of the theater scene there. He was intimately involved with several independent theater houses, and was visiting the family property in Ohio this weekend, scouting fresh talent for two of his soon-to-be-released off-Broadway productions. He was the person who had orchestrated the entire three-day workshop we were attending and brought in all the presenters and performers. Having put together my own small-scale seminars for the college drama department, I could appreciate what a huge undertaking his project really was. On the other hand, I didn't pay much attention to what June was saying. I had heard most of it before, and the majority of it was even true.

"Well, thank you ladies, for the enjoyable conversation this evening. I hope this was your first stop because there's still plenty of time for you to enjoy the park's attractions, even if you're planning to attend tonight's theater presentation. The park doesn't close until midnight on the weekends." With a final flirtatious grin aimed in June's direction, he was gone. He hadn't even mentioned the incident in the theater.

Chapter Fifteen

O thou invisible spirit of wine, if thou hast no name to be
known by, let us call thee devil. ~*Othello*

Our waitress had been noticeably absent the whole time
Gabriel was sitting with us, but as soon as he left, she
appeared at our table with two more glasses of wine. "Is there
anything else I can get for you? Your bill has been taken care of,
so take your time and enjoy."

June hesitated for a second as Sasha placed the drinks in
front of us. "We didn't order these. Oh what the heck. I'm sure
they're from Gabriel." She still had that moony-eyed look on
her face, but she wasn't about to refuse a free glass of good wine.
For that matter, neither was I.

"So now what? I sure hope you don't feel like riding any
roller coasters because this time I refuse."

June gave me a look. "Seriously, Francie?"

"Geesh. Now you sound like Hamm. Let's take the scenic
boat ride back to the hotel. The last time I was on that ride was
about ten years ago with Hamm and the twins. It was fun, but

I'm sure the whole thing has changed over the years. I think there were pirates and skeletons back then. Most likely, we'll see zombies this time. In any case, it might be a good place to unwind and regroup after this crazy day."

"That's fine, as long as there aren't any clowns. I'll take the undead over the unfunny any day."

The floating attraction was nearly full by the time we made it to the front of the line just before its scheduled departure time. We were able to get the last two side-by-side seats by the portside railing and settle in just before the boat pulled away from its mooring. The pilot performed a running commentary of the sights as we leisurely motored up the river. "Look to your left, and you will see the site of the park's newest ride, the Daredevil. It is the tallest and fastest coaster in the world. It was built just last year as one of the many new and exciting additions to the park." Everyone on the boat craned their necks in unison. We looked like a line of synchronized lemurs.

"And on your right you will see the cottage where the marina manager makes his home." Our guide made a weak choking sound when he realized what he had said. Obviously, he was reciting from a memorized script, and rather than making matters worse, he just let it go. People around us began whispering and pointing toward the attractive rustic home. Apparently word was already getting out about the recent crime, and just in case any of the passengers didn't notice the guide's slip-up, a long yellow streamer announcing Crime Scene was waving in the evening breeze for all to see. At least no one was pointing at us in accusation.

"Look, June! Did you see him?"

"Who? Where?"

There was a light on in Bob's house, and I swore I saw Eddie Sneed in the window. Who else wore a garish Hawaiian shirt and a pet squirrel on his head? He walked past the window again and turned on another lamp in what looked to be the living room.

June stuck her head over the side of the boat. "I see him. You're right. No doubt in my mind that it's Eddie. Lend me your phone and I'll try to get a photo. I left mine on its charger back in the room."

By the time I located my phone among all the other important stuff in my bottomless bag, we were too far up the river to get anything usable.

"Now what do you think that was all about? He's been gone since before lunch and shows up now? What business does he have in Bob's house?"

"Whatever it is, it can't be good." Before I could continue my train of thought, I looked down at my phone screen which had lit up while I was still holding it. Hammond's smiling face looked back at me.

"Are you there? Francie?"

"Oh, hi, Hamm." I quickly held the phone up to my ear. I must have inadvertently dialed him up while digging through my purse a minute ago, but he didn't need to know the call was not intentional.

"Are you girls having fun? I can just imagine the stories you'll have when we see you on the Fourth."

"Nothing too exciting happening over here, just the usual seminar stuff." (fingers and toes crossed, checking pants to make sure they're not on fire)

"Well, Jack and I had a great day on the course, an excellent dinner, and now we're just about to have a drink and smoke a cigar."

"I'll let you go then, Honey. I think my reception is cutting out. Talk soon. Love you!"

June was staring at me. "Did you just lie to your husband? You never lie to your husband."

"That's why I had to hang up. I realized I didn't want to draw him into this sordid mess unless I had a solid reason to do so. You were right before. He sounded like they were both having a great time. Why spoil their weekend?"

As promised, the boat ride ended at the side entrance to the hotel. On our way back to our room, we passed the theater, where *Much Ado About Nothing* was resuming after its intermission. I peeked in the theater thinking it might be fun to catch the final act, but then all I could see in my mind was that disturbing series of film clips I was trying so hard to forget and the equally strange sight of the out-of-place stealth clown. Suddenly, I no longer had any desire to watch a Shakespeare performance, in fact, I couldn't wait to get into the hotel room and bolt the door.

Chapter Sixteen

When shall we three meet again in thunder, lightning, or in rain? When the hurlyburly's done,/When the battle's lost and won. ~*Macbeth*

"So now what?" June and I were secured behind the locked door of our room, but I realized it was still relatively early, and I wasn't the least bit tired. There was still too much adrenaline flowing through my system. "We could watch a movie. We won't even have to pay for it."

June rolled her eyes at me. Come to think of it, it was a pretty lame idea. If June had suggested it, I would have treated her to the same response. "Okay, then, what do you suggest?"

June plopped onto her bed and clasped her hands under her chin. "I can't shake the thought that something is very wrong where Eddie Sneed is concerned. First the guy practically moves in with us. Annoying as he was, I don't see him just backing off because we asked him nicely. Plus, he wasn't anywhere he was expected to be this afternoon, most noticeably in the theater when we were treated to that filmfest starring the terrible trio. I wouldn't have minded so much or even thought about it again, but then he shows up at Bob's house in the woods?"

"Are you thinking what I'm thinking?"

"Do I need to answer that?" June was already in motion. She was pulling a black fleece over her head and unplugging her phone from the charger. The cute shoes she had worn to dinner were gone and black velcro-close sneakers had replaced them.

Not to be outdone, I did a quick-change worthy of the best stage actress. My ensemble was now black leggings, black ballerina flats, and a long-sleeved black T-shirt with the Phantom of the Opera logo artfully displayed on the front. Operation: Find Eddie Sneed was officially under way.

I used the room phone to dial up the courtesy shuttle that ran twenty-four hours picking up and delivering resort guests to every destination in the complex. "I need a ride to the marina, please."

Families with tired, sunburned children, teenagers in love, groups of friends out for a good time, all entered and exited the resort shuttle as we made our way around the vast property. Only one or two riders gave us more than a quick glance. Two ladies dressed all in black were not by any stretch the strangest sight anyone would see tonight. When the shuttle bus stopped in front of the marina office, it was finally our turn to get off. We were the only people in the immediate area since the office was closed for the evening, and I had to wonder who was filling in for Bob tonight. It was just after dusk and lights glowed invitingly all along the docks. The view into the amusement park from our vantage point was noteworthy. Roller coasters laughed in technicolor and the streets were lined with cheerful lampposts. Who wouldn't want to vacation here?

I stood still surveilling our location. "There must be a road leading to the house somewhere nearby. Bob would have insisted on getting to and from work without hassle. Let's head around to the back of the building."

"There it is, Francie. They did a good job concealing the road from the public area, but it's not like it's a secret path or anything. We can walk it easily, but we better be on the lookout for cars. It was clearly built for motor traffic."

It took under five minutes to reach our destination. There was still a light on in the quaint house, and by the day's last rays of sunshine, I could see the neat green lawn and the trimmed bushes under the picture window. I was having a hard time envisioning Bob tending the flowers and yard, but then figured that a maintenance crew must have been part of the package deal.

"Quick!" June grabbed my arm and shoved me into the brush beside the road. We were in a stand of cottonwood trees which could potentially be a bad thing if I was supposed to be quiet. If I stayed under this tree more than a minute or so, the snowy fluff falling from the branches would launch me into a sneezing fit I would be unable to control. I looked in the direction of June's wide-eyed gaze and sucked in a huge gulp of air, along with a few fluffy cottonwood seeds. "What the..." I managed to wheeze and willed myself to swallow back the inevitable sneeze. There was no mistaking the pair rushing away from the cottage hand-in-hand. Angelina's golden hair shone in the emerging moonlight, and Damien, well, Damien was just impossible to mistake for anyone else.

Had they been inside, or had they arrived at the house and seen Eddie there? And why was everyone so hyped up about getting into the home of the late Roberto DeVille in the first place?

We remained very still for what felt like a long time, waiting and watching until we were sure the DeVilles weren't coming back or that no one else was following them out. "Aah...choo!" I couldn't hold it in any longer. I doubled over at the waist and sneezed violently about twelve times in a row. "Sorry. I have allergies."

"Oh, I know." June looked out past our hiding place and cautiously stepped around the trees and back onto the road. "Come on. The coast is clear. But can you please be quiet?"

I found a tissue in my bag, gave my nose a good blow, and followed June. To say I was glad to get away from the offensive trees would be an understatement.

We crept up to the house, avoiding the large front window, and sticking to the shadows until we were safely crouched beneath one of the side windows of the living room. Of course, we peeked inside.

Chapter Seventeen

'Tis one thing to be tempted, another thing to fall. ~*Measure For Measure*

Eddie was sitting on an ugly green plaid couch with a big cardboard box on the floor between his feet. He was concentrating on something he was holding, but I couldn't tell what it was. After staring at the item for a few seconds, he put it back in the box and withdrew a square piece of paper, it looked like a photograph. "Aah...choo!" I looked apologetically at June and shrugged my shoulders. What else could I do? Eddie stood up and looked nervously around the room. I wasn't sure if he heard me or not, but he dropped the photo back into the box and made for the back door.

We waited a few minutes, making sure Eddie wasn't just taking a potty break or getting himself a glass of water, then made our way cautiously around to the back of the house, where we found the kitchen door left open in the wake of Eddie's hasty departure. "We might as well go have a look inside. It wouldn't be breaking and entering after all."

June agreed. "Technically, we would just be entering."

Walking through the small functional kitchen, we got a glimpse into the private life of Roberto DeVille. There was a single stained coffee mug in the sink, a take-out bag containing an uneaten hamburger and some cold fries on the counter, and one lonely chair tipped over in the middle of the room, away from the worn table. I instinctively reached down to set it right, but then realized I might be walking through evidence and pulled my hand back, leaving the chair where it lay. I made a point not to touch anything as we passed through the kitchen into the living room. "It looks like Bob's dinner was interrupted. I wonder what really happened in the middle of that awful storm?"

I didn't get any further into my musings, because June had made it around the couch, dropped to her knees in front of the big cardboard box, and let out an alarming yelp.

"Francie, this is awful. This is..." She stuttered unintelligibly and then clamped her mouth shut. June was so seldom at a loss for words that I was afraid to see what she had found. It was more alarming than anything I could have imagined.

I didn't see anything too disturbing at first. It looked like the box was filled with a variety of electronic storage devices from cassette tapes to CD's, DVD's, and flash drives. There were some older cameras—the kind that were considered cool until cell phones became as good as or better than the average camera. Also strewn among these items were various connector cords and a few items I didn't recognize. I had the sense they were parts of surveillance equipment, probably based on things I had seen on TV.

But then I saw what had silenced June. I gently took the photo she was still holding and stared agape at the likenesses of the three clowns from the video. The way they were dressed, there could be no mistake. It looked like it could have been taken at a Halloween party, but wherever they were, their distinctive monochromatic outfits were a sure giveaway. I held the photo close to my face, trying to get a closer look at the red clown with the scared eyes, hoping to find a clue as to his identity. When nothing registered, I dropped the offensive picture to the floor and began scrutinizing the rest of the contents of the box.

There had to be at least a hundred photos in the bottom of the box. In addition to the three stars of the film, there were pictures of traditional-looking clowns making balloon animals on the causeway, passing out candy to children, and wait, what the heck, removing a wallet from an unsuspecting father's back pocket. Flipping through a stack, I found another clown with another park visitor and another seeming act of theft.

"Wow, June, snap out of it and look at this stuff. Bob has pictures of klepto-clowns in here. Do you think this is the 'proof' we're supposed to get?"

June did snap out of it and began rifling through the box. She found a CD labeled with a date from last summer written in permanent marker. "Put this in your purse, Francie. We'll look at it when we get back to the hotel."

I hesitated, realizing we were probably tampering with evidence, but only for a fleeting moment. I grabbed the CD, along with a number of the photos, and stuffed them in my purse.

"Wait a minute. Hand me that photo of the girl in front of the roller coaster. I know her." June handed me the photo and I was dismayed to see a former teacher's assistant smiling proudly in front of the roller coaster she operated during summer break. "I don't think she was aware she was being photographed, any more than any of these other people."

"Look closely, Francie, there in the background." June pointed to two men dressed like park employees, standing off to the side. One was holding a bag, the other had a wad of cash in his hand. They were making an exchange of some sort.

The more we looked, the more photos we discovered that pointed to surveillance throughout the entire resort complex. It seemed many park employees had been caught on film engaging in less than legal activities.

We bounced questions and theories at each other and after a while, a possible understanding of the pile of evidence in front of us began to take shape in my brain.

This information gathering obviously had been going on over a long period. Bob had likely been spying on just about everyone at the resort, and it seemed probable that when he came across evidence of people committing crimes or indiscretions, instead of alerting security, he chose to use the photos for his own purposes. Maybe he was blackmailing the clowns, and now that he was gone, they wanted the evidence of their wrongdoings destroyed.

June dropped the photo she was holding and watched it flutter back to its place among the rest of the artifacts. "Maybe he really was crazy. I can't picture him being a stalker, but your idea about blackmail makes sense. In any case, this is one big box of creepy."

I noticed the pulsing blue lights out on the driveway right before I heard the short bursts of the police sirens being turned on and off. Feeling a sense of dread, I threw the photos I was holding back into the box while June gathered up the ones on the floor and did the same. Then I stood up deciding to face whatever was coming next head-on. They didn't knock. I heard the hard footfalls of thick leather heels on the front porch approach and then recede. They entered through the kitchen at the back of the house, just as we had. I wondered who had called the police? It wasn't us, and it wasn't like we were the only intruders into Bob's house of horrors that night. Someone was trying to set us up. Or were they trying to protect us from something? My head was starting to hurt again. It was getting hard to tell where we fell on the "who killed Bob" spectrum.

The next hour and a half was a blur. Detective Reed and Officers Rymer and Stark took turns rifling through the disturbing assortment of evidence in the box and posing the same questions over and over to both of us in every imaginable form.

Chapter Eighteen

Let no such man be trusted. ~ *The Merchant of Venice*

We were hauled off to the police station and cited for trespassing. We were questioned yet again, fingerprinted, (for elimination purposes), and then unceremoniously deposited back at the hotel.

It felt good to be back in our nicely appointed room once again, but by this time it was beginning to feel more like a prison. I finally admitted to myself that after one murder, three encounters with the police in under two days, and evidence that June and I were the objects of someone's sick joke, that this was not going to be the relaxing retreat I had hoped for. I desperately wanted to call Hamm and have him spirit us away in the middle of the night and never return to Devil's Island, but I knew that nothing would be solved that way. I made up my mind. Let the police do their thing, but it was going to be up to me and June to figure out what was really going on.

"I don't know about you, but I don't plan on sitting around here waiting to be arrested for killing someone I don't even know well enough to hate. I mean, Bob was annoying, but I never gave him much thought outside of the marina."

I got no argument from June. She grabbed the pad of hotel stationery and the complementary pen, sat in the desk chair, crossed her legs, and declared, "Let's review."

Point by point, we ticked off each of the strange events in the order in which they occurred. We made note of all the main players. First there were Bob, Angelina, and Damien DeVille. Next we met the young resort employee, Sasha, and Gabriel DeVille, and finally there was Eddie Sneed.

"Francie, give me the CD from Bob's house. Let's see what's on it."

June fired up her laptop while I dug for the CD. I handed it over and she popped it into the computer which immediately began making unhealthy-sounding whirring sounds. After about ten seconds of this, a box with an error message popped up on the screen. "Files unreadable. Files may be corrupt."

I was disappointed, but not particularly surprised, especially when I saw the deep scratch across the surface of the CD. It wasn't in a case when I tossed it in my bag, so I couldn't tell if it was already like that or if it had met its demise in my purse. Next, I retrieved the photos and we scrutinized them for clues. Neither of us recognized any more people, but several of the images showed couples locked in steamy embraces, and other guilty-looking individuals caught forever glancing over their shoulders. Somehow all of these events and people were connected.

"I say we start with Eddie. He seems to be the most approachable, and he sure seemed eager to hang out with us, that is, until he disappeared and showed up at Bob's house, with his hands all over that surveillance stuff."

"Umm. Our hands were in that cookie jar too."

I looked down at the photographs strewn across the coffee table. "Whatever."

June shook her head at my lame response as she looked over her notes and jotted down a few more observations in her own investigative reporter shorthand. "Let's go, Francie. There's no time like the present. If we're going to do this, let's do it."

" Yes, okay, but let's call Eddie's room first and see what he has to say for himself. I'll call the front desk and have them connect us to his room."

Eddie answered on the first ring. "Oh my gosh! I'm so glad you called. I have to talk to you. It's really important. You might be in trouble, but I can't talk here. Where are you? Did you see them? Are you guys okay? We need to meet. I have to show you something. You're not going to believe this."

"Slow down, Eddie. Take a breath. We're not buying the bumbling idiot act any more. If you don't want to talk here, let's meet in the park. It's public and no one should notice us, if that's what you're worried about."

"Yes. Good plan. Leave right now and meet me by the fun house. It's close to the entrance, and there shouldn't be a lot of people around at this time of night." I shared what Eddie had said, and we both agreed that we didn't have a whole lot of choices at the moment.

He was already there when we arrived. Glancing over his shoulder once, he ducked inside. Great. I never did like fun houses. Once, when I was about thirteen, I got to visit a local carnival as part of a class field trip. After admiring my reflection in the infinity room, proudly circling so I could see my budding curves from every angle, I got disoriented and then separated from my group of about a dozen other students. By the time the attendant located me, I was curled up in a tight ball, arms around my knees, tears leaking out the corners of my locked eyelids.

The emotions of that day washed over me as I stepped over the threshold. Mirrors covered every surface, distorting our images into grotesque beings worthy of my nightmarish memories. I was hanging on to June's arm with both of my hands, and I'm pretty sure I wasn't breathing. Strobe lights pulsed and flashed, pushing the terror deep into my pores. Seeing my condition, June stepped up to the plate and dealt with Eddie.

"What's this all about, Sneed? This better be good. I'm in no mood for games."

"No games, I promise. I just didn't want to be overheard or followed. You need to know..."

"Not again!" We were pitched into utter darkness, which oddly made me feel better. I didn't have to deal with my crazy fears, and sadly, I was getting used to flailing about in the dark.

Chapter Nineteen

In time we hate that which we often fear. *~Antony and Cleopatra*

"Okay. This isn't so bad," I said bravely. "The entrance should be right behind us. We didn't walk in very far." I turned and faced the way we had come and stretched my arms out in front of me. I had to flex my fingers as they were a little numb from hanging on to June. I took a step forward and touched a solid wall. I must have miscalculated. I ran my hand across the wall to the left. Nothing. I repeated the action to the right. More nothing. It was as if the entrance had sealed itself once we were inside. Probably a special effect, forcing unsuspecting thrill-seekers to keep moving forward, finding their way out through the maze of mirrors, no turning back. I wasn't feeling brave any more.

"Click, click, click. Click, click, click." Moving around in the dark had me disoriented. I couldn't tell from which direction the sounds were originating. I turned slowly in a circle, stopping after every step and listening. The clicking sounds were there, at the same intensity, no matter which way I faced. They got louder and faster, and then I felt something scuttle across my foot. A lot of somethings. June screamed. At least I knew I wasn't alone.

There must have been an emergency generator, because as suddenly as we had been immersed in total darkness, we were plunged into a garish circle of white light. Correction. June and I were in the middle of the spotlight; Eddie Sneed was nowhere to be seen.

What I did see were hundreds of tan, brown, and fluorescent green skeletal creatures clicking their pincers greedily in every direction. Their multiple eyes darted blindly about while their tails slapped venomous stingers in scary, staccato rhythms. The clickers turned out to be scorpions.

"Help! Help! Somebody get us out of here! Sneed, you little creep, where are you?"

Twirling and shaking my legs like a ballerina on amphetamines to avoid contact with the bloodthirsty insects, dizziness threatened to overtake me. Reflections of reflections spun around me making me feel like I was in the belly of a crazy kaleidoscope.

"Gabriel, is that you?" I heard June scream in the middle of a revolution. It crossed my mind that she might subconsciously enjoy the role of damsel in distress. Not me. I just wanted out. I continued to scream and hop and twirl until at last, I heard a third voice in the space, a loud male voice, devoid of panic. It was not Gabriel.

"Who's there? What's going on in here? Hey, who are you two, and where did all these scorpions come from?"

I was amazed at the calm demeanor of the young park employee standing in the open doorway that now was exactly where it should be. "Look out! These things are poisonous!"

"Sorry to alarm you ma'am. They sure as heck look scary, but they're not lethal. At least I'm pretty sure they're not. This isn't the first time a plague of scorpions has rained down upon us here."

Who was this kid, all calm and Biblical-sounding? And was there a good reason I should take his word about all this?"

He got between June and me and placed a steady hand on each of our shoulders. As he calmly led us out into the warm night air, I remembered Eddie. "Did you see a short guy in an ugly Hawaiian shirt when you came in? He was the one who led us in here in the first place, but when the lights went out he disappeared."

"Sorry. I didn't see anyone coming out. I just heard you two screaming. I placed a call in to the police, then came in to see what was up."

June joined the conversation. "You called the cops? Great. Wait a minute. If Eddie didn't come out, he's probably still in there. Do you think he was on the level? He could be in trouble. We should get him out."

The young man, Curtis, according to his name badge, held up both his hands. "Whoa. nobody's going anywhere. Let's just stay right here until the police come, and they can sort all this out."

As if on cue, the now all-too-familiar blue lights appeared, and two out of three of our new best friends got out of the car. Detective Reed looked as fresh as if she had just stepped out of the shower, while Officer Stark was still rumpled, runny, and stuffy. Officer Rymer must have had the night off. Lucky him.

Reed stepped forward, all official and no-nonsense, pen poised above paper. "Ladies, I understand you encountered some difficulty in one of the attractions this evening."

Really? Some difficulty? "I think being locked in a deathtrap and attacked by killer insects should be classified as something a little more serious than 'some difficulty.'" I couldn't help myself, even though I realized I probably wasn't earning any brownie points in the law enforcement world.

"Stan, why don't you go inside and look into the scorpion situation. I'll stay out here and get these ladies' statements."

He didn't object, but it was clear he was thinking, "Oh, sure, send me in to be poisoned."

Stanley Stark shuffled toward the fun house entrance. He greeted the scorpion infestation with an onslaught of violent sneezes. Hundreds of scary little bug legs were probably high-tailing it to every available nook and crevice in the place.

After listening to each of our versions of this latest misadventure, Reed looked over her notes and tucked her official notebook tidily into her pocket. "Okay, here's how I see it. The entire resort has been experiencing black-outs and electrical problems since yesterday's storm. We're away from the main power plant in town, so it can take a while to work all the bugs out after a storm." Her lips turned up at the corners. "No pun intended."

"What about the scorpions?" I didn't understand why no one seemed particularly concerned with the fact that we had been attacked by a marauding cyclone of bloodthirsty creatures.

"It's an ongoing problem, Francie. I'm not trying to downplay your concern, but this is likely the handiwork of a group of pranksters we've been trying to pin down for years. You may be familiar with Scorpion Island. It's only a few miles from here, and the source of many rumors and urban legends. Some folks find it amusing to stir up allegations of mafia activity on the island and like to frighten locals and visitors alike with tales of underworld crime, sex trafficking and other undocumented claims. The scorpions have shown up before around the park. Holiday weekends are especially popular. I'm sure Officer Stark will confirm my theory that your uninvited visitors are quite harmless, although nevertheless alarming."

I could sense June's natural curiosity bubbling to the surface; unfortunately, it was accompanied by her snarky sarcasm. "Thanks for the clarification, Detective. That's all very interesting, but what about Eddie? I don't think the harmless scorpions spirited him off to their parlor for a tea party."

Evelyn Reed was nonplussed. "Of course, you're right. We will locate Mr. Sneed just as soon as we drop you ladies back at your hotel. I would suggest that you stay there this time."

We reluctantly got into the all too familiar back seat of the cruiser, and as soon as Officer Stark returned from his mission, no worse for the wear, we were once again escorted back to the main entrance of the hotel.

Chapter Twenty

Some rise by sin, and some by virtue fall. ~*Measure For Measure*

How many times were we going to leave this room in search of answers just to be escorted back to the hotel entrance by the police? The questions were multiplying and although there was a seed of a theory taking shape, we were getting no solid answers. Someone was involving us in their less-than legitimate activities, and we just kept spinning in circles getting nowhere.

June headed straight for her laptop again. She was used to diving into Internet research, but I was not. I preferred to talk through my problems, but the person I most wanted to talk to was probably sinking his teeth into a thick, juicy steak right now. That thought made me realize I was hungry. I also needed to wash the remnants of Bob's house and the police station off my tired body, so I headed for the room service menu. A snack would help me restore a sense of normalcy, and after all, it was on the house. Having a hot bath and a little something to eat would help me focus and clarify my thoughts.

I found some delicious-looking pepperoni-and-cheese-stuffed breadsticks and a very nice California red blend on the menu. June discovered some interesting information about Scorpion Island on the Internet. I listened to her findings from behind the partially-open door of the bathroom where I decided to take advantage of the luxurious whirlpool tub, especially since there were wide marble ledges all around the tub, perfect for holding a snack plate and a wine glass.

"Did you know that there are only sixty residents on the island and they are all members of an exclusive club? Looks like everything on the island is controlled by this club including real estate purchases. If you want to become a member, a current member has to quit, and you need recommendations from at least two other members. What do you say, Francie? It will only cost you around $150,000 for your membership plus monthly maintenance fees."

"Why not? Put my name on the list. I'm sure they have a nice golf course, so Hamm will have no problem." I sipped my wine and munched thoughtfully on the last bite of my yummy breadstick as I listened to June's commentary about the mysterious island.

"Not only is there a golf course, but there is also a health club, a pool, and several bars and restaurants. And of course, there's a boutique with all sorts of exclusive merchandise. It says here there's even a tattoo parlor run by some famous Russian artist. He specializes in scorpion tattoos."

"Of course he does." My thoughts wandered back to Memorial Day weekend and two beautifully-executed, mirror-image scorpion tattoos belonging to a set of gorgeous twins, Sirena and Senora Divine. Sadly, the first one was murdered by the second one, who then tried to murder June and me.

"On second thought, June, I think I'll keep my money. I'm really not a big fan of scorpions, real, tattoo, or otherwise."

"You have a point, Francie. Neither am I." June continued to share her research findings as she came across more interesting facts. "The summer staff on the island comes mainly from Eastern Europe. There are about a dozen men and the same number of women who live in separate dorms. They're trained to recognize the residents by their appearance and also by the yachts they arrive in. Holy cow! I think it would be stressful to have a job like that."

"I bet those people are not easy to work for."

"No kidding. You wouldn't want to stop by unannounced either. If you come in on a boat that isn't recognized, you won't even be able to dock. There are security guards patrolling the entire shoreline on land and in boats, and it doesn't specifically say so, but this article makes it sound like they might be armed. In any case, they aren't open to tourists. No wonder there are so many rumors and myths about this place. Sounds like the perfect place for high class crooks to come for a little privacy and R and R."

"Thanks for the geography lesson. I think I'll stick to South Bass and Middle Bass Islands. And Kelleys of course, as long as Senora is still safely behind bars." I shuddered at the thought of the crazy lady who had nearly made our Memorial Day weekend trip the last vacation either of us would ever take. I leaned back into the soothing whirlpool tub, set my wine glass on the wide marble ledge, and closed my eyes.

As I was drifting off to sleep, I could hear June talking. I only caught her end of the conversation with, I presumed, her editor. Her voice was low and muffled by the bathroom door, but I got the gist of it. She was asking her boss to do some digging for her to see how much truth there was to the rumors of crime bosses and mafia ties to Scorpion Island. I'm pretty sure I heard her mention Chicago and a potential anonymous source.

I woke up long enough to drag my water-wrinkled self out of the tub, throw on my pajamas, and head to bed, but, as so often is the case, once I was all snuggled under the covers, I was wide awake. My mind raced, and I tossed and turned, willing myself to fall back to sleep, with no success. I finally got tired of watching the clock tick off the minutes, and at 5:45, I got up, changed into yoga pants and a T-shirt and decided to take a walk on the beach to think and clear my head.

Chapter Twenty-One

Best safety lies in fear ~*Hamlet*

The sun was still at least a half hour away from making its morning appearance when I began my wandering trek down the shoreline. It wasn't exactly dark because the lights from the resort and park cast the beach in a comforting glow. When I was all alone at times like this, it was easy to believe that everything would be all right. I had almost convinced myself that today would be a new drama-free day. I picked up my pace and was content humming "I Will Survive," along with Gloria Gaynor and my iPod when a whistling sound shot past my ear and the sand in front of me shot up like a volcano eruption, leaving a crater in the wet mud. I changed directions and picked up my speed from a brisk walk to a full-on run back toward the hotel. Another sand explosion erupted just to my left and I realized I needed to get out of the open. As much as my brain fought against the idea, the reality was that someone was shooting at me. I scanned the beach for some kind of cover. The closest thing I could see was the tiny beach office just outside the hotel. I think I set a new personal sprint record as I ran for cover, all the while repeating the mantra "I will survive" in my head. I made it to the office and pulled at the door handle praying that it would open. Someone up above was clearly watching over me as the knob turned easily in my hand and I ran inside, slamming the door behind me. I leaned heavily against the door, doubled over hugging my waist, and sucked in as much air as my burning lungs could hold. After several more deep breaths, I inventoried my body for bullet holes, and finding none, I began crazily pushing buttons on my phone, willing it to do my bidding. Another shot rang out, connecting with the wood just outside the door. I tucked myself snugly beside the door frame away from either of the two windows and finally managed to steady my breathing and speed dial June. At least that was my intention. Hamm's smiling face appeared on my screen. Uh-oh. Wrong button.

"Good morning, Sweetheart! You're up and about early. I'm so glad you called. You'll never guess what happened after I talked to you yesterday. I won a hundred dollar gift certificate to Bay Harbor. We can have dinner there for our anniversary."

"I'll call you back, Hamm."

"What? Wait."

I didn't have time to explain or feel bad about hitting the disconnect button. I placed my forefinger deliberately on the second icon in my favorites list and pressed.

"Mmmmm?"

"June!"

"Yeeah, iz me."

"June, wake up. It's Francie. Someone is shooting at me down on the beach. Call the police."

"What?" She sounded clear and alert now.

"Call the police June! I'm being shot at. I'm in the beach office just outside the hotel."

"Oh, okay."

"What do you mean, okay? Get help!"

The line went dead. All sounds from outside stopped as well. I inched along the wall to the edge of the window facing the beach. Should I take my chances and look out to try to see who was after me, or should I dial 911? The sound of shattering glass interrupted my decision-making moment. I only had time to punch in 9 before I noticed the smoke billowing out from beneath a storage closet door. The gravity of my situation struck me as explosions split the air. I almost missed the small, strained voice coming from across the room.

"Fireworks. Those are fireworks."

"Who's there?"

There was no answer, but I recognized the voice. I crouched down remembering my stop, drop, and roll, and staying below the sulfur-tinged smoke, I made my way across the room and peered around the reception desk.

"Angelina, are you okay?"

She didn't answer. The air was heavy with the noxious smoke. Soon there would be nowhere safe left in the small office. Fireworks had been stored in the utility closet, but now they were hissing and bursting against the thin panelling of the adjoining wall. I had to get us out, and fast.

It appeared that Angelina had been hit on the head. She was barely conscious as I struggled to help her up from the desk chair and out the door. The weight of her limp body leaning on me plus the oppressive smoke was almost more than I could stand.

"I've got all my life to live, and all my love to give and I'll survive, I, I, I will survive..."

"FRANCIE, WAKE UP!"

"Turn off the alarm June."

"Francie, thank God. You're okay."

"Is it time to get up?"

"Francie, don't you remember the fire? You were trapped in the beach office with Angelina, and the fireworks stored there somehow ignited."

"Oh, that's not good. Is it time for breakfast?"

When my eyes finally focused in on June, I could see that she was wearing a pair of men's plaid boxers and a ribbed tank top with her hair spiked up in all the wrong places. She had my purse and her knapsack crossed over her shoulders and her laptop clutched to her chest looking like she had left the hotel room in a rush. I was on a blanket on the sand, not snug in my downy bed. The private beach of the resort was filling with sleepy-eyed, disoriented guests, forced out of their own beds at the insistence of the shrieking fire alarm summoning them so rudely, diverting them from their sweet dreams.

The sea of sleepy hotel guests in various states of dress and undress were inching closer to the small aluminum-sided office, chattering, questioning, speculating about what had happened. It was slowly coming back to me. I was in the office when the fireworks exploded. Something had caused a spark that lit the fuses. Now I remembered. It was a gun, a gun directed toward me. The more alert I became, the more fear and panic tried to overtake me.

Sirens from the fire trucks at the scene still competed with the hotel's fire alarm for most migraine-inducing sound of the morning. I massaged my temples, trying to remain calm. I watched the firefighters as they went about their business. Some stood at attention, hoses aimed like muskets at the fiery enemy. Others, armed with shields worthy of the best medieval knights, stormed the small office, well-protected from the kamikaze missiles, rockets and shells that would have made for a memorable Independence Day celebration, but in this context, managed only to call up images of an air raid from an old war movie. I tried to stand up. I needed to get away from here and whoever was using me for target practice. When I wobbled to my feet, the stars I saw were not from the fireworks. I slumped back down to the blanket and waited for the wooziness to pass.

The buzz of speculation wound down, and the hotel guests were given the all-clear to return to their rooms. The novelty was wearing off, so one by one, the onlookers turned from the spectacle and walked back toward their own lives.

June and I watched for a few more minutes as the firemen wrapped things up. I finally convinced the hovering medic who kept trying to shove an oxygen mask onto my face to go find someone else to bother. I was feeling much better, physically, at least. Other than a dry throat and a few bouts of coughing, I was okay. My emotional state was another matter entirely. I felt like I was hanging on by a thread. What else could possibly happen? Just when I decided the answer was nothing, I was once again surrounded by my three least favorite people. Officers Stark and Rymer stood off to the side flipping through notepads and glancing at their watches while Detective Reed began the questions. I could sense her frustration as once again I had no answers for her. I didn't see anyone on the beach. I didn't know where the shots had come from, and most of all, I had no clue who would be using me for their morning target practice. She was gentler with her interrogation than during our previous encounters, as I'm sure she could see I was trembling and didn't want me to lose it on her watch. I was beginning to think the lady might have a heart. She confirmed that there was, in fact, a bullet retrieved from the splintered wood near the office door and that it would be analyzed, but that did little to assuage my anxiety or to answer the question of why I was being targeted in someone's disturbing game of cat and mouse.

When her questions were finally exhausted, and she was satisfied I didn't need medical attention and would not be leaving the resort, I weakly suggested to June that we do the only thing I could think of at this point. "Let's head back to the room. There's no reason to stick around here. I was hoping to start this day off with some peace and quiet, but this is about as far away from calm as it could get, and to tell you the truth, the sight of a burning building brings back memories I'd rather not revisit." Not nearly enough time had passed since June and I had been locked in a burning warehouse full of counterfeit designer merchandise instead of an arsenal of fireworks and narrowly escaped our own premature demise. Just the sight of this fire was making me very uncomfortable. June put her steady arm around my waist and gently guided my steps back toward the hotel.

"There's nothing left to see here people."

Nothing left to see, but plenty left to think about. June was quiet and so was I. The walk was providing me just the right mental backdrop to try and sort some things out. What was Angelina doing in that storage building, and who was using me as their morning target practice? Angelina had been taken away in an ambulance before I could talk to her. As much as I prayed she would be all right, I also needed to see her and find out what she might know about what was going on. I didn't like that my name was being mentioned in connection with a fire for the second time in as many months.

Chapter Twenty-Two

Can one desire too much of a good thing? *~As You Like It*

When we got back to the hotel, my first thought was to go back to our room, crawl under the covers and hope for a do-over. I changed my mind, however, when the hypnotizing aroma of strong cinnamon-infused coffee tickled my nose. I spotted the coffee shop at the same time I caught a glimpse inside the sparkling display window of *She Devil*, the most exclusive women's apparel boutique in a twenty mile radius. I nodded my head in the direction of the gourmet coffee and bake shop, and June did nothing to dissuade me. We placed orders for cinnamon bun lattes and a tantalizing variety of freshly baked pastries with the unenthused barista and took them out to the porch that encircled the entire perimeter of the hotel. June fought me for the sticky bun, but we both laughed when we realized since it was roughly the size of my head, it was big enough to satisfy us both.

I was finally starting to feel more, but not quite, like my old self. Looking across the courtyard at the inviting aquamarine water of the pool, I had an epiphany. "June, we haven't been ourselves. If we're ever going to get to the bottom of this murky mystery, we are going to have to step it up."

I knew that the best ideas my friend and I ever had evolved over either sinful foods or extravagant spending, so I decided we needed to crank it into high gear, Francie and June style.

"Soak up that caffeine my friend because we are about to work out our credit limits."

"I like the way this is headed Francie. What are you thinking?"

"I'm thinking we don't step one foot farther into this resort until we relieve *She Devil* of two amazing swimsuits, cover-ups, and some fabulous coordinating accessories."

"Now that's the kind of workout you're not going to have to talk me into."

Side by side we stepped over the threshold into shopping paradise. As if on cue, a retro remix of "Brown-Eyed Girl," came on over the speakers. It was "our" song. Hamm sang it to me on our second date, and it's been part of our special history ever since. I couldn't resist grabbing a handful of ridiculously expensive and skimpy swimsuits to try on in a *Pretty Woman*-style fashion show medley.

I'm certain the shopkeeper was annoyed by the guffaw and giggles coming from the dressing room as we modeled the suits that looked perfect on the mannequins, but not so great on our real life figures. Finally the stuffy retail clerk called a stop to our exploits. We were told to choose a purchase or go find the nearest Walmart to continue our shenanigans. As much as I was offended by her snooty insinuation, I couldn't pass up a darling halter suit with a black and white polka dot top and a red skirted bottom. Hamm was going to love me in it as long as I intercepted the credit card bill before he saw it. June also handed her American Express card over for a black, one-piece, strapless suit with a white, appliqued cat's face across the entire top. On anyone else it would have looked ridiculous, but on June, it worked.

Having completed our first mission, I had one more shopping emergency to conquer. I needed something shiny.

Not even a full hour after my terrifying flight for life on the beach, I was feeling much more in control of myself and my surroundings.

"Next stop, poolside breakfast and mimosas."

"I like the way you think. I really thought you would be making a beeline for the nearest cab to get you off this island by now. But I can see you're determined to prove them all wrong. I'm proud of you, Francie."

The poolside area was deserted at this hour except for one painfully pink man whose protruding belly just screamed for aloe. We chose a seat very far away. A blue and white cabana on the south side of the pool had not yet been reserved, so I whipped out my buzzing Master Card and secured it for the day.

"I don't know about you June, but I'm all about some quiet time to soak up some sunshine and process these last couple of days."

We got comfortable on the cushioned loungers and slathered on the sunscreen. (We didn't want to end up looking like our pool mate.) The morning sun felt rejuvenating. I took an extra moment to admire my new ankle bracelet embellished with a tiny anchor charm as it sparkled in the sunlight.

"Is it too early for nachos?"

"I think they are still serving the breakfast menu Francie, but nachos definitely sound like a plan for later."

The waiter brought our pitcher of mimosas and our breakfast out to the cabana just as June got her iPad booted up and connected to the hotel wi-fi. I settled for a fruit and cheese plate which turned out to look more like a party platter. Six different kinds of cheese with mini croissants and a nice selection of the freshest fruits in season. I was in breakfast heaven. June also looked pleased with her selection of banana nut silver dollar pancakes and orange slices (a healthy choice for sure) with maple dipping sauce. It was nice to sit quietly and enjoy the simple things in life.

When I had my fill of cheese and felt a comfortable glow thanks to the mimosa, I decided it was time to get down to business. Research was June's expertise, but I can navigate Facebook, Twitter and Google like a pro. It was time to get my cyber-stalk on and find out more about the people we had met so far.

Twenty minutes later, I was back to popping cheese cubes into my mouth more out of frustration than a renewed hunger. "I hope you're having better luck, June. I think we have come upon the last group of people in America who don't make it their life's goal to post, tweet or update on everything they do. I can't get anything on Angelina and Damien beyond legal documents regarding their real estate purchases and a marriage certificate from fifteen years ago. Same with Gabriel. Just a bunch of professional pages for his theater group. I did manage to find a clown group based in Sandusky, but all I accomplished was accidentally making a donation to their balloon fund. Are you having any luck?"

I looked over to gauge June's progress, but she was asleep, softly snoring while her iPad screensaver twirled and displayed the time. I gently nudged her shoulder to wake her up. It was time to pack up and get to our first workshop of the day.

Chapter Twenty-Three

If you prick us do we not bleed? If you tickle us do we not laugh? If you poison us do we not die? And if you wrong us shall we not revenge? *~The Merchant of Venice*

"**O**kay, Day. Bring it on." June was fueled up, rested, and ready to go. "I think our first session is pretty appropriate, considering."

"Hmmm? What's that?" I didn't even recall what we had signed up for.

June held the flyer out toward me, pointing to our selection which she had circled in purple ink. I took it absentmindedly, making a mental note that my friend constantly amazed me with her penchant for color-coordination. Her ink pen was the exact shade of violet as the streak in her spiky blond hair, which in turn matched the shade of her body-hugging mini dress. Her lime green tennis shoes were the finishing quirky touch that gave June her unique style. She could pass as Tinkerbell's modern counterpart.

Theatrical Weapons and Combat Staging was scheduled to begin at 9:30 in room 384. "Seriously, June? Do you think we could pick something else? I'm not feeling the whole 'weapons and combat' thing. After this morning, I'm not sure that gunslinging is at the top of my to-do list."

"It might be exactly the right thing, Francie. Come on. Maybe fighting a make-believe assailant on the stage will help you remember more of what happened on the beach. Maybe you'll even figure out who it was."

I reluctantly agreed, mostly because I couldn't think of anything better to occupy the next couple hours.

"Great, Francie. Anyway, there are other weapons besides guns being demonstrated according to the blurb. Maybe we'll end up in a swashbuckling pirate scene. The seminar was about to start, so all we had time for was a bagel and a banana on the fly, not that we were hungry, but it's so hard to pass up free food. The room was filling up quickly, and we had to maneuver our way through knots of people before finding two seats together. We ended up having to squeeze past four seated attendees and taking two open spots in the middle of a row very near the back of the conference room. No sooner had we settled ourselves in our chairs, than the earsplitting screech of microphone feedback assaulted our ears.

"Sorry about that. Welcome everyone. If you could all find a seat, we can get started." Our presenter stood at the podium in front of the room, tapped several times on the mic, and fiddled with the controls on the side of the wireless device, adjusting the volume.

I'm not sure why I was surprised, but I hadn't expected this session to be led by a woman. I fished my itinerary out of my bag and scanned the list until I located the information I wanted: Theatrical Weapons and Combat Staging, presenter–Dr. Alex Covington. Shame on me for assuming Alex plus weapons expert equaled man. Dr. Covington was not especially tall, but her straight posture and fit frame combined to make it clear that she was not a lightweight. She wore straight-legged black pants and a sleeveless black stretchy top that showcased her well-defined arm muscles.

"Ladies and gentlemen, we have some great activities in store for you all, but before we can get started, there is some very important safety information we need to go over." Several assistants in hotel uniforms walked down the outside aisles with stacks of handouts, handing them to the people in the end seats to pass down the row. I heard a few groans as the packets were handed from person to person. When I got mine, I scanned the information and recognized a lot of it as the same safety and accountability guidelines I had used in the past. While the others were skimming the reading material, I took in my surroundings. We were in a typical, convention meeting room, but a few modifications had been made to facilitate this session. The front of the room was transformed into a split-stage; props were utilized to create a simple, wide staircase to the left and two floor-to-ceiling mirrors on the right. Interesting.

"Oh, great," June huffed. "Just what we need."

"What now?"

June had also finished reading through her packet, and was scanning the room. "Don't look now, but we can forget about worrying about Eddie Sneed's whereabouts and safety. He's just across the aisle and one row behind us. We're going to have to question him about Bob's house and the funhouse fiasco, but it will have to wait."

Of course I had to turn in my seat and gawk. The nerve of that little weasel to just show up as if nothing had happened. June placed her hand on my knee, preventing me from hopping up and causing a scene. I was going to have to bide my time, but he wouldn't slip out of my sight this time. "Okay, fine, but I've got my eye on him, and I will be getting answers before any of us leaves this room."

"Firearms employed for theatrical uses, must be treated as though they were actual live-firing weapons, and the rules for safe firearm handling, as well as plain common sense, should always be observed." Covington read the words out loud, and I went back to pretending to dutifully follow along. She paused for effect and scanned the audience, making sure we were taking her words to heart. Then she continued.

"The gravest errors that can occur in the handling of stage weaponry originate from an inappropriate sense of complacency." Again, she stopped to highlight the seriousness of her words.

"I will be your weapons coordinator. This means I am in charge of all weapons. It is my responsibility to keep them secure between scenes and to maintain and control all blank and dummy ammunition. I will instruct and assist the actors who will handle the weapons, supervise loading, firing, and unloading, and, above all, oversee the staging and choreography of the scene and the safety of all who will be involved." June whispered to me, "This is a lot more serious than I thought it was going to be. I feel like I'm back in high school."

"Give it a few minutes. The instructor is required by law to recite all of that. I've heard the same introduction more than once. Once she finishes the formalities, the interesting part will begin. Maybe I'll even get the chance to shoot that traitor, Sneed." June smiled at my enthusiasm.

"Okay. There's just one more thing we need to do before we get started. If you all would turn to the last page of your packets, read the release of liability clause, and print and sign your name on the lines provided, and pass the forms to the end of the row, one of my assistants will collect them. We'll get everyone confirmed, and then we can get on with a little murder and mayhem." A smile spread slowly across Dr. Covington's face, lighting it up like a proud mother at a toddler's recital.

I tried to get into the spirit of the session even though I was a little less excited after having been shot at for real less than three hours ago. At least I knew there was no threat with all of the safety protocol in place. Maybe June was right and going through the motions might actually help me figure out what had happened on the beach and who was after me.

We were put into two groups. Attendees to the left of center stage would participate in a sword fight scene from Romeo and Juliet, while the other half of the room would be using pistols to reenact the final scene from Orson Welles' film noir, *The Lady From Shanghai*. June and I ended up in the latter group.

"Oh, darn. I was kind of hoping to be in the sword-fighting group. Those swords look pretty awesome, and I wouldn't mind doing a little swashbuckling." June flourished an imaginary sword for effect.

"Now that we're here, I'm kind of warming up to the idea and I think you're going to like this scene, June. There's lots of action and intrigue; it's not just a matter of point-and-shoot."

I was more excited than I would have imagined to be put in the group performing *The Lady From Shanghai*. To sweeten the deal, I was selected by Dr. Covington to play the role of Elsa, the female lead in the production. I had a secret love of the film noir genre, and this particular film, based on the novel, *If I Die Before I Wake,* by Sherwood King, was one I had watched many times, admiring Rita Hayworth's dark portrayal of the gorgeous Mrs. Bannister. The bizarre yachting cruise and the complex murder plot captivated my imagination right up until the final scene which takes place in a hall of mirrors, not unlike the one from the funhouse we were trapped in last night. Come to think of it, the memory of the ending of this film probably triggered my overactive imagination and elevated my sense of dread and panic at the time.

Dr. Covington handed scripts to the twelve people in our group so everyone could follow along with the scene. Realizing that Eddie had just accepted a script from Alex, I snatched my own copy from her hand, making myself appear rude. I hoped she didn't change her mind and reassign the lead to someone a bit more appreciative. She shot me a stern look but thankfully that was the extent of her reprimand. I glanced at the typed pages in my hand and set them aside.

" Don't you even want to read the script?"

"Call me a stage geek, but I pretty much know these lines by heart. There are some variations between the screenplay and the novel, but I've got this. I'm more concerned about keeping my cool having to work with Eddie on the scene. That will be the true test of my skills. At least I can keep my eye on him until I get the chance to get the truth out of him."

"Well, aren't you Miss Celebrity Actress? You shouldn't have any problem staying in character, though."

"Yeah, I guess. It's what I do, except I'm usually on the other end, being the instructor. It will be fun to get to play the role of stage actress for a change. I haven't had a lot of time to get involved in community theater outside of the college lately. Funny, I thought once the twins went off to college, I'd have all kinds of extra time to join in local productions."

Sometimes I fumbled and stumbled through the crazy stuff real life hurled at me, but there wasn't much on the stage I felt I couldn't conquer. The room was buzzing with excitement. People were vying for positions within their groups and trying to make themselves noticed for the roles they wanted to play. Between the adrenaline and the testosterone flying around, I felt like the hormone level in the room could hold its own against a room full of menopausal and pregnant women. We all were itching to get started on the weaponry demonstrations. Alex, as Dr. Covington asked us to call her, set down the cup of steaming coffee she had been sipping while the groups acquainted themselves with the scripts. It was almost time for me and the two others selected to be in this introductory activity to get our firearms and head up to the staging area to perform our mini-scene.

Alex made her way back to the podium. "At this time, I need everyone except for our first two groups of performers to take their seats." She had to make the announcement twice before the buzz of excitement in the room began to fade and everyone made their way to their seats. I stayed up front and scanned the room to see where June was sitting so I could make sure she would have a good view of my performance. Every once in a while it was nice to be the center of attention and show off my skills for my friend, since, through no fault of her own, she found herself in the spotlight more often than not. As that thought skimmed my consciousness, I finally located her, not sitting with the other participants waiting to observe me and my fine acting skills, but upstage left, tucked in the corner in a perfect Weaver Gunman Stance, right leg slightly back, allowing for accuracy to the target and a smaller profile to present to an attacker. None other than Gabriel DeVille's body was wrapped snugly around hers, his hands covering her hands, demonstrating the move. She caught the raised eyebrow look I was throwing in her direction and stepped quickly out of the circle of Gabriel's arms. The spell was broken when she realized everyone was moving to their seats, so she headed across the makeshift stage toward the short set of stairs. At the bottom of the third step she turned to give me a thumbs up in encouragement for my upcoming role, and almost collided with that sneak Eddie who had apparently wandered behind the scenes and was now creeping back out trying not to be noticed. That's hard to do while sporting a hideous hibiscus-decorated Hawaiian shirt and the ever-present orphaned opossum headdress. He sidled up to me all nonchalant like I hadn't even noticed he was gone. And then, the room was once again in an uproar. There was a loud crack overhead. I looked up and saw one of the spotlights dangling precariously by its cord right above Alex. I ran to where she was standing, oblivious to the danger, and shoved her out of the way just as the large spotlight broke free and crashed to the floor. Alex staggered away from her podium and tumbled down those same three steps to land in a limp heap at June's feet.

Chapter Twenty-Four

Ah, kill me with thy weapon, not with words! *~Henry VI*

Gabriel and I were the first to reach her. He was already on his cell phone dialing 911. I bent down and cupped Alex's head in my hands. I could see that she was still conscious. Her forehead and upper lip were beaded with sweat, and her ankle was turned at a very unnatural angle. The resort's emergency medical responders rushed onto the scene just moments after Alex's fall. After checking her vital signs and posing a few questions to the people in the immediate vicinity, the medics helped Alex stand with their support, and she was ushered out of the room.

Gabriel stepped up to the podium and took control of the conference session. I'm sure he was beginning to rethink taking on this whole convention scene, as the weekend was certainly not going according to plan thus far. In an effort to get the participants back into an organized and orderly state, he stepped up to the podium and announced, "May I have your attention everyone? Let's please settle down and allow the medical staff to assist Dr. Covington. In the meantime, I will be taking over the role as weapons coordinator. Let's try to focus. I hate to sound cliche, but the show must go on. I put in a call to the hotel maintenance and they are going to make sure everything is secure with the lighting system. Until they give us the okay, look over your lines and I will start getting the stage weapons ready. I'm sure there's no cause for alarm, and we can go ahead and continue our lesson."

After a few minutes of readjustment, the participants were ready to get back to work. It was amazing to me how people could just brush by the ugly and misfortunate plight of others as long as they had other things to keep them occupied. I, on the other hand, wasn't quite ready to sweep this newest accident under the rug. The string of mysterious events taking place at this conference were feeling less like unlucky coincidences and more like parts of an organized agenda. Whose agenda it was, and its desired outcome remained to be seen.

Gabriel distributed each actor's weapon with a few additional reminders about safety and technique. My character, Elsa, used a Colt 1908 vest-pocket nickel semi-automatic pistol with a two-inch barrel and a lovely pearl grip. The gun felt heavier in my hand than I imagined the ladylike replica would have been.

Due to time constraints, both groups were going to have to perform their scenes simultaneously. I figured it would work out all right since it was the choreography and weapons demonstration that we were focusing on rather than the actual dialogue. Besides, I was just excited to play my role and experience the little high I always got from being at center stage. I must admit, I am a bit of a drama diva.

Gabriel cleared his throat. "Silence, please!" His commanding voice had the desired effect. The audience waited in hushed anticipation.

Then came the familiar command, "Action!" I felt like I was poised at the starting blocks of an Olympic relay waiting for the gun signal. The performance began.

I was transported in my imagination to a dark hall of mirrors where I stood in a black dress, perfectly composed and aiming my Colt directly ahead at the mirror image of myself. I was Elsa. The clanking of swords and the words from the actors portraying Tybalt and Mercutio just feet from where we were working were completely drowned out as I focused on the voice of the man portraying my deceived lover reciting his lines from just beyond my field of vision. It was a voice I had come to know recently—not that of a jilted lover, but rather one that sent waves of apprehension, frustration, and pent-up anger pulsing through my bloodstream. It was the voice of Eddie Sneed, but the familiar grating sound now carried a darker undertone. Did he have unexpected acting skills, or did he possess a true element of danger?

"With these mirrors, it's kind of difficult to tell. You are aiming at me aren't you? I'm aiming at you, lover. Of course, killing you is killing myself. It's the same thing. But you know, I'm pretty tired of the both of us."

I barely breathed as I anticipated the deafening sounds the blank shots would make when we fired at the images of ourselves in the mirrors. My hand was steady with my finger tensed on the trigger waiting for the three second count from the last word spoken until I fired my weapon. I inhaled and held my breath, feeling the anticipation and the adrenaline, knowing that a gun was aimed directly at my chest, even though it was not loaded with live ammunition. And then the screaming began.

I instinctively squeezed the trigger of my gun when the first scream pierced the air. The blank round firing was deafening, but I was still able to hear the sound of shattering glass behind me and the shouts all around the room. I tried to sort out what was happening in all of the chaos. On the other side of the stage, one of the male actors was lying on the ground clutching his leg. Blood was oozing through his fingers where it seemed he had cut himself while wielding his sword. Although dulled, the swords are still blades and can cut if you aren't extremely careful. People from the audience flooded onto the stage to help him. I was about to go lend a hand myself when it registered that the mirror behind me was shattered, and shards of the reflective glass were still raining down onto the stage floor. How had the mirror broken? We were firing blank rounds at each other, but there was nothing and no one else around me to have caused the mirror to shatter. Unless.... the round being fired at me hadn't been a blank.

Chapter Twenty-Five

Our doubts are traitors, and make us lose the good we might oft win, by fearing to attempt. *~Measure For Measure*

After the fiasco in the conference room, there was nothing else Gabriel could have done other than cancel the class and dismiss early for lunch. It was a beautiful, summer day, the kind of day a person should be sitting on the beach or anchored out in the bay, not eating lunch out of a bag in the courtyard, wondering what all of the recent accidents and coincidences had to do with us.

"It's a good thing we haven't had to pay for anything this weekend because the only things we've gotten our money's worth on so far is catastrophe." June took a thoughtful bite of her turkey sandwich. "I wonder how Angelina is doing. I meant to ask Gabriel if he knew."

"It probably slipped your mind, being wrapped in his arms, and all." Oops, my snarky side was rearing its sarcastic head.

"Hey, he was just showing me the proper way to effectively aim and shoot a pistol."

"I bet Jack could have shown you how to do that if you were really interested." The look on June's face told me I had gone too far. "I'm sorry. That was mean. I'm just feeling out-of-sorts. First Eddie disappears from the funhouse, then conveniently shows up as my partner in a shootout with blank ammo that shatters glass. And then we have Angelina turning up semi-conscious in a burning building, one, might I add, in which I was taking cover from real-life bullets, and now Dr. Covington is whisked away in an ambulance."

"And don't forget Bob."

"Ugh. Bob. Somehow it feels like Bob is smack in the middle of all of this. Everything seems to have cycloned since his murder and this investigation. I cringe every time I think about that box in his house."

"And the clown videos in the theater."

"And nearly getting sawed in half." My head was starting to hurt. Instead of finding out what or who was at the root of all of these strange goings-on, things were getting exponentially worse. This was not turning out to be the relaxing, fun getaway we had planned.

My mental rewind was cut short when June pointed toward the gazebo in the middle of the commons area. Whatever she said, I had no idea because her mouth was full, but she obviously thought something couldn't wait until after she swallowed, and she wanted me to see it right away. I directed my gaze in line with her pointed finger, scanned the grassy area, saw lots of people enjoying sunshine, snacks, pets, and other summertime activities, but nothing out of the ordinary. Finally she gulped, coughed, waved her hand some more and said, "Over there, it's Damien. Come on, maybe we can find out about Angelina." Like it or not, I was going, since June had a death grip on my arm, propelling me up and toward Damien.

I had a chance to take in his appearance before we reached him. He was still Heathcliff handsome, wearing black jeans and black T-shirt fitted in all the right places. On second thought, I was not opposed to speaking to him.

When we approached Damien, he was standing statue-still, hands clasped behind his back (did I mention Heathcliff?), staring off in the direction of the charred beach office. His expression was unreadable. I debated whether we should just walk away and leave him to his musings, but June settled the debate before I could weigh the pros and cons.

"Hi, Damien. How are you doing? How is Angelina? Is she going to be okay?" June fired questions at Damien in rapid succession. The image of Eddie Sneed flitted across my mind. Did people find June and me as annoying as Eddie? Yikes. Note to self: think before speaking, or at least try.

Damien looked up slowly, acknowledged June with a nod, then fixed me with his dark eyes. Something about the way those eyes bore into mine sent a shiver from my hairline to my tailbone. I got the disturbing feeling that he was accusing me of something, but what, I did not know.

"She's resting comfortably. She was overcome by the smoke and lost consciousness for a short time, but aside from some temporary memory loss, she'll be fine." He wouldn't look at me, and it was starting to get on my nerves.

"Damien, what is it? If Angelina is okay, what's bothering you? Did she tell you something?"

"It's not so much what she said," he answered in a low gravelly voice, "it's more the unanswered questions and strange accidents that keep piling up ."

He looked pointedly at me again. Did Damien think I had something to do with her being in the office when it caught on fire? June was scrolling through messages or statuses or emails on her phone. Either she had some brilliant idea or she was dealing with all of this in a wildly inappropriate manner. She looked up from her screen and said, "Don't look now, Francie, but I think this party is about to be crashed."

Chapter Twenty-Six

This above all; to thine own self be true. *~Hamlet*

Damien and I both looked up and saw Detective Reed heading toward us. His shoulders slumped, and I felt something stirring deep in the pit of my stomach that I recognized as dread. I had been relieved to escape another round of accusatory questions after the episode in the theater, but it seemed my luck had run out. Reed did not bother with formalities. "Mr. DeVille, I just spoke to your wife. You should probably go home. She's feeling better and wants to be with you."

I didn't think the lady could crack a smile but there it was. Her face lit up, and her eyes twinkled and crinkled at the corners. She was downright pretty. I nearly let my guard down and relaxed, but when she looked at me, the smile left and so did the mood. "Ms. Egge, I need to speak to you."

I sat down hard on the wraparound cement bench that encircled the inside of the gazebo; more because my knees were beginning to shake so badly I didn't think they could support me than to signal my immediate agreement to speak to the detective. Damien and June both backed away and stepped down from the gazebo. I sent a quick pleading look in June's direction; unfortunately, Detective Reed stepped forward and blocked my signal for help. She sat beside me with her elbows on her knees and stared straight ahead for what seemed like forever. I couldn't take the uncomfortable silence for another second. My nerves were shot and I thought I could feel my left eye beginning to twitch.

"I didn't have anything to do with the fire, Detective. Or Bob's murder, or the accident on the stage. I don't see why you're wasting your time tracking my every move when the real criminal is running rampant on this island and needs to be stopped." I felt a little more in control having started the conversation rather than always responding to the implied accusations of the detective.

Detective Evelyn Reed continued to stare out past the horizon. She was so still and so intense; she seemed to be fighting some internal battle. Finally, she released a long breath and turned to look me in the eye.

"Listen Francie, I've thought long and hard about this investigation. The bottom line is that crimes are being committed, and it is my job to follow the leads and the evidence to find out who is committing them. My dilemma is that all of the evidence is shaping up to implicate you, but my gut is telling me that you are innocent."

"I am innocent. You should listen to your gut. Your gut sounds very reasonable to me."

A small chuckle seemed to take Reed by surprise. I could sense that this conversation wasn't easy for her. Confiding in me was making her very uncomfortable. She started speaking again in almost a whisper, so I had to tilt my head very close to hers to make out her words.

"As I said before Francie, I have to follow the evidence. I'm sure you have noticed that the evidence, although very circumstantial, continues to point in your direction. I may be chasing a ghost, but my hands are tied. There is more going on here than what is showing on the surface. There are powerful people in this area who have their own endgame in mind, and they know how to cover their tracks. They also don't care who they take down in the process. I'm not authorized to go on a wild goose chase, as my captain calls it, based solely on a hunch or a gut feeling. I can't tell you anything else with much certainty, and I can't condone any vigilante justice, but it might be in your best interest to have your friend dig a little deeper into the Scorpion Island angle she was looking into."

"Do you mean that the mob is behind these crimes?" I couldn't believe what I was hearing.

"I told you all that I can. Just be careful, and don't trust anyone." With that said, she stood and walked away, leaving me feeling like I had a heavy weight fastened to my chest and was being pulled ever-so-slowly to the bottom of the lake.

I was still sitting there like a petrified log when June came back and took the seat that Detective Reed had just vacated.

"What did she say to you? What's wrong, Francie? You look like you just saw a ghost."

"Jimmy Hoffa's ghost maybe. Come on June, we need to get back to our room. I can't breathe out here." I started speed walking back to the hotel, for once not caring if June followed.

I just needed to get out of the open and process what I had just heard.

"Slow down Francie. What has gotten into you?"

June caught up to me just as I reached the door and burst inside like the devil himself was on my tail. As soon as she crossed the threshold, I slammed the door shut and secured both locks as well as making sure the Do Not Disturb sign was hung on the knob. My frenetic mood was not slowed down by the confines of the room. I paced back and forth like a wind-up toy that was wound too tight.

On my third trip around the room, I flicked on the TV and cranked the volume as high as I could. Only then did I feel safe to repeat the detective's words and warnings to June.

After listening quietly, which wasn't easy for her, June agreed with me that there was more going on here than met the eye. She agreed with Detective Reed that we should dig deeper into the rumors surrounding Scorpion Island. Maybe it really was a hideout for organized crime. I had to admit, it was the perfect setting, secluded and luxurious, for crime lords to plot and plan their evil agendas. But what did it have to do with me?

I sat down in one of the matching conversation chairs in front of the closed draperies. Next to me, scattered about on the table, were pamphlets, menus, and itineraries for all the workshop events, as well as the attractions and restaurants throughout the resort. Peeking out from under the pile of papers, I spied the glossy red all-inclusive passes trimmed in gold that Angelina had given us on our first day of the convention. I remembered that the world-renowned Heaven's Gate Spa was included in the amenities.

"Let's skip the afternoon sessions and take a trip to the spa," I suggested. I think we could both use some extended quiet time to organize our thoughts. I held up the passes for June to see, then tucked them into the inside pocket of my handbag which was still slung crossbody over my chest. She nodded in agreement. Although it was still early, recent events had me feeling mentally drained. It was time to regroup.

Chapter Twenty-Seven

I like this place and willingly could waste my time in it. ~*As You Like It*

We got off the elevator on the ninth floor where the spa was located. Stepping through the frosted glass double doors, we entered into the peaceful zen world of the Heaven's Gate Spa. Soft melodies and soothing scents infused the air, and the muted grays and soft greens of the furnishings added to the tranquil environment.

"Welcome ladies. May I assist you with your visit this afternoon?"

"Hello. We don't have an appointment." The receptionist's serene expression puckered, but before she could scold us for being so presumptuous as to appear before her unannounced, she spied the VIP passes I had discreetly removed from my handbag and now held casually in front of me.

"Oh, of course. If you would like to review our list of services, I will be more than happy to arrange a schedule for your afternoon."

We had already decided on luxury relaxation massages with facials, and I informed Alina (I could read her gold name badge now) of this. She wrote some things on two green tickets, handed them to me, and instructed us to follow the long hallway to its end, turn right, then enter the main salon at the end of the corridor where we would be greeted by a personal attendant for a complete tour of the facilities and further directions to our destination.

I felt the tension drain from my body as we made our way down the quiet hall. About halfway down, we passed a floor-to-ceiling water feature, making a hypnotizing, rippling murmur that had the immediate effect of soothing my jangled nerves. Finally, at the end of the hall, we came to a stop in front of a wall covered in glossy river rock. To the left and right of the rock wall were identical frosted glass doors leading to separate private wings, presumably one for women and one for men.

I didn't notice any obvious indication of the proper entrance choice. "June, does it say anything on your ticket about which door we should enter?"

"There's a number at the top, G-135, that's about it. What about yours?"

I looked closely at the green ticket in my hand. "Mine says G-136 at the top. Seems pretty generic to me."

"Wait. Look closely, Francie. There are letters etched into the glass. The left one has a D, and the right one has a G. Didn't that receptionist say to turn right?"

"I'm not sure if she meant the hallway or the door. Let's go right. G probably stands for girls, don't you think?"

"Sounds good to me." June opened the door and in we went.

"Oh, look at this amazing hot spring pool."

I looked over to the raised marble platform just in time to see a man facing away from us, getting ready to step down into the steamy tub. He dropped the towel around his waist and lowered himself into the water. There was absolutely nothing between his skin and the swirling steam. Did we run, scream, laugh? Oddly, no; we casually continued walking down the hall as if it were a perfectly mundane scene. It wasn't until we encountered a second gentleman (thankfully, this one was wearing a spa robe) coming out of the locker room that it dawned on me something was amiss.

"Since when did they start letting women into this wing of the spa?" the robe-clad man asked.

Another man, this one fully-clothed in neatly-pressed, spa-employee attire, approached us, gently took both of us by the elbows, and escorted us back the way we had come, politely pointing out that the ladies' wing was directly across the hall. Once alone outside, we stood there for a beat then crumpled into wheezing laughter that brought tears to my eyes and folded June over at the waist.

"What the heck just happened? Why didn't we turn and bolt after seeing naked hot-tub guy?" I had to wipe my eyes and take a deep breath before I could continue. "I think my brain must be fried."

"We both just acted like it was the most natural thing in the world," June added.

"It actually was the most 'natural' thing in the world. I'm just glad those guys didn't make a big deal of it. It could have been really embarrassing."

June gave me a look. "I'm pretty sure this qualifies as pretty embarrassing."

"Well, I think the doors should have been more clearly marked. Those letters were hard to see and pretty ambiguous at that. If G doesn't stand for girls, what is it then? And what does the D stand for?"

June's eyebrows came together as she thought aloud. "Gabriel and Damien? Obviously not. Girls and Dudes? We know that can't be it. I've got it. Gents and Dames."

"I guess that makes sense, but why didn't they just use nice standard labels like Men and Women? Serves them right if there are mix-ups. I'm sure we weren't the first ones to make that mistake."

We were given a thorough tour of the women's facility by a lovely Russian girl named Polina who spoke in the distinctive accent of so many of the Devil's Island employees. After showing us the wide array of hair and nail services, hot and cold pools, steam rooms, and saunas, Polina led us through the locker room with private changing rooms and into the large waiting area. She recited the names of all the hot and cold beverages on hand and told us to help ourselves to fresh fruit arranged in silver bowls on a long table against the wall. Before she left, she handed us a menu card with an extensive list of other food and drink options available. All we had to do, she told us, was to pick up the phone on the side table and make our request.

We had about an hour to kill before our massages were scheduled. Snuggled in our fluffy white robes, we opted out of using the naked pools and whatnot and decided to check out the snack menu.

"How does sushi and chardonnay sound?"

I looked up from my menu. "You read my mind. You know what they say about great minds thinking alike." June's smile was bright and genuine as she walked over to the side table where the house phone was located, grabbed a shiny green apple, and placed our order. She bit into the apple, sunk into a comfy upholstered chair and stretched her legs out in front of her. She was the picture of relaxation, at least for now. I was curled up in the corner of the couch with my legs tucked under me and was also starting to let go of the tension of the last day and a half.

"This was a much better idea than attending a lecture on period hairstyles, don't you think?"

"Most definitely. Now maybe we can relax, clear our minds and come up with an explanation of why the cops keep hounding you." June took another bite of her apple and chewed thoughtfully.

"Where do we start? Bob is hounding us from beyond the grave. I'm afraid to find out why he had a box full of creepy surveillance in his house. And how does Eddie fit into this picture?"

"And I'm getting the sense that there are things we don't know about our hosts, like why Angelina and Damien were at Bob's house in the first place."

"We were there too."

"Then Angelina shows up in the burning beach office just in time to pass out."

"Plus I was shot at. Twice." I didn't want to give in to my frustration because that would defeat the whole purpose of being here, and since I felt like we weren't getting any closer to putting the puzzle pieces together, I decided to check out the fruit bowl across the room. I nearly had a head-on collision with the person delivering our snacks.

"Excuse me, I'm so sorry," we said in unison. I recognized that soft Russian voice immediately. "Sasha! It's you again. Do you work everywhere in this resort?"

"I go wherever I am told. Many of us are trained in many jobs to prevent problems if someone cannot work their assigned schedule. I will just leave this tray here. Enjoy your stay, ladies." And with that she was gone.

"I guess her explanation makes sense, but these surprise appearances of hers keep adding to the feeling that we're missing something." As I tried to quiet my running internal monologue, I fixed a plate of sushi, poured a glass of wine, grabbed a napkin, and returned to my spot on the couch. June followed suit, tossing her apple core in the trash and piling her own plate with as much as it could hold. She had to set the plate down to pour herself a glass of the perfectly chilled chardonnay.

This was more like it. We relaxed in the luxurious lounge, savoring the delicious California rolls and enjoying a second glass of wine. I needed to remember the name and vintage so I could purchase another bottle or two when I got back home. I was thinking I wouldn't have been opposed to closing my eyes and drifting off for a few minutes, so when a soft voice brought me gently back to the present, I realized I had done just that. It was an attendant coming to collect June and escort her to her masseuse. The pretty, dark-haired girl informed me that my personal assistant would be by momentarily, and before she and June were out of the room, my eyelids were growing heavy once more and sleep was beckoning to me. I welcomed the invitation to catch up on some much-needed rest and gave in without resistance. The lilting voice that woke me for the second time was a now-familiar one. When I opened my eyes, Sasha stood in front of me holding out her hand to escort me to my appointment.

"Miss Francesca, if you will come with me, I will show you to your room. There has been a slight change in the schedule, but not to worry. Oksana will take excellent care of you. She is the very best therapist in all of the spa."

I followed my guide like an obedient puppy down the long quiet hall, still a little groggy from my interrupted nap and that extra glass of afternoon wine. All the doors had small whiteboards attached to the outside. About halfway down, we passed a closed door with a magnet affixed to the whiteboard proclaiming the message, "Reserved for our VIP guest." Underneath the magnet, written in a flourishing cursive hand, was June's name. The next door had an identical magnet, and underneath the VIP tag was my name written in the same fancy script. I stopped and was about to go inside when Sasha directed me a little further down to a room with no magnet and no name on its door.

"We passed my room, Sasha. My name is on the door right next to June's room."

"Yes, as I mentioned, there was a slight schedule change and you will be with Oksana in this room. You should be honored. She only works with our very best customers. Relax and enjoy your time here." She ushered me into the well-appointed room and left me to undress and slip under the silky soft sheets to await the arrival of the wonderful Oksana.

I was not disappointed. For the next hour, I gave in to the magic of her hands, breathing in the soothing smells of essential oils, listening to cerebral music, and giving my tight muscles over to the restorative strokes of my therapist's expert touch. Of course, it couldn't last.

June's frantic voice startled both Oksana and me. I popped up from the massage table, wrapped myself in the sheet, and bolted out the door. The yelling was coming from the room that had my name on it. "What's going on? What's the matter? What happened?"

June was standing next to a woman I had never seen before, but her dark curly hair looked disturbingly familiar. Her hands were at her throat, and she was wheezing.

June zipped past me and headed out into the hall. "Did you see anyone come out of the room? A man?"

She was straining her eyes in the opposite direction from where I had come.

"No, I didn't see anyone. What's going on here?"

June looked from the stranger to me. "I'm not sure, exactly, but I got here just in time."

The lady with the bouncy brown curls regained her composure, slipped into her complimentary robe, grabbed her clothes, and stopped for just a moment, locking eyes with me, before leaving the room. "I'm going to find security and report this. That man was not a masseur. If he was, he was awfully rough. He nearly choked me. If your friend hadn't come in here and startled him, who knows what might have happened." And with that, she was gone.

For the first time since entering the room, I got a good look at June. She was dressed in her own clothes, and her hair looked amazing. Of course, no one else on the planet could pull off her style, but that's what made it all the more beguiling. The color was lighter than it had been this morning. It looked like a platinum halo encircling her head, shimmery little spikes sticking up like mini sparklers tipped in various shades of gold.

"What the heck have you been up to, June? And again, what's going on in here?"

"Well, when my massage was finished, I was told you got off to a later start, so I decided to take advantage of a few more free services." Her hand shot up to finger her masterful new 'do.

"I can see that. Whoever styled your hair was a genius. And speaking of hair, did that lady's hair look too much like mine, or what?"

"That's just it, Francie. When I was finished, I came back to find you. I looked in the obvious place—the room with your name on the door, and when no one answered my knock, I peeked inside, only to see some goon with his hands around your neck. Correction, someone who looked an awful lot like you from behind."

"I was moved to a different room at the last minute. Do you think that guy was really trying to hurt that lady?"

"It looked like it to me. It also looked like he might have mistaken her for someone else." June's angelic face was marred by a shadowy veil of fright. I imagine my own face had lost its glow of content from just a few minutes ago. June followed me back to my re-assigned room so I could get out of the sheet and back into my own clothes.

"I think we better talk to Sasha. She must be able to tell us something. Let's find her right now and get to the bottom of this."

"I can't argue, Francie. Sasha has to know something, and she's going to have to tell us what."

I finished dressing and checked the mirror. My hair would have to stay in its state of unwieldy curls for now. This was war. Well, not technically war, but I was up for a good face-off. June swiped her fingers through her hair, and now it looked more like her version of a warrior headdress than a halo.

We retraced our steps through the facility, popping our heads into the locker room, stepping into the various pool areas, and finally opening the door to the sauna. We found who we were looking for. Sasha was slumped sideways on the cedar bench; she did not appear to be napping.

I shook her gently, trying to wake her up just in case she really had dozed off, but since she was still dressed in her work uniform, this was unlikely. June felt Sasha's pulse and lifted her head gently looking for signs of foul play. After determining that she was breathing and was not bleeding, we lifted her from either side and shuffled her out of the hot room. Since there was no place to sit in the hall, we helped her back to the lounge and lowered her onto the sofa. I brought her a cup of water and held it to her lips.

Her eyelids fluttered and her gaze ricocheted about the room trying to get her bearings.

"Find her please. Please help her. They have her on the island."

"Help who, Sasha? Who has her? Where?"

June approached her and asked, "What were you doing in the sauna? Did someone hit you? Did you see him? Are you in some sort of trouble? We can't help you if you don't tell us what's going on."

I could barely understand the poor girl. She was still disoriented and looked terrified. Her hand was at her throat, thumb and forefinger rubbing an antique locket that hung from a thin gold chain around her neck. I offered her another sip of water and waited for her to calm down so I could get some information. I really wanted to ask her if she knew anything about why my schedule and my room had been changed at the last minute, but she was in no condition to be grilled, so I waited. Her thumbnail triggered the tiny latch on the locket and it popped open, revealing two photographs. I thought at first they were both pictures of Sasha, but when she held it out toward me in her trembling hand, I bent closer to see that the likeness on the left was indeed her, but the picture on the right was a younger girl who looked very much like her but with darker hair and piercing green eyes.

"Is this your sister? Is this who you are trying to find?"

Just when it looked like she might be ready to carry on a productive conversation, she sat bolt upright, her eyes fixed on the entrance. Angelina made her way into the lounge and sat down right beside Sasha. "Are you okay dear? I saw you sitting here as I was passing." She reached for Sasha's hand which was now resting limply in her lap. "You have been working too many hours on too little sleep. Why don't you come with me, and I'll make sure you get back to the dorm safely. I'm going to have a word with your supervisor about cutting back your hours." Sasha did not object. She got woodenly to her feet.

Angelina directed her next words to June and me. "I find myself apologizing once again for my staff causing you any inconvenience or disruption to your plans. Sasha is a good girl, but she sometimes stretches herself too thin in her enthusiasm to earn money over the summer. I'll see that she gets back home safely and takes it easy the rest of the evening."

I wasn't willing to let it go so easily. "Wait a minute, Angelina. I was just about to ask Sasha a few questions."

"I'm sure it can wait for another time. Obviously, she's not feeling well."

"Speaking of feeling well, how are you feeling? You had quite the scare yourself in the beach office. I'm surprised to see you back at work so soon."

Angelina blinked her eyes rapidly. "Thank you for asking. It was a freak accident for sure. I should be asking about your well being though. You were there too, and I must thank you for helping me out of the building. I've been telling Damien for months that we need to find a safer place to store the nightly fireworks, somewhere far away from populated areas. At least the huge stash for the Independence Day show is safely stored where there can be no accidental detonation. We'll be getting out of your hair now so you can relax. Enjoy your visit here at the spa. I'll see you both very soon." Angelina guided Sasha away, one hand on her shoulder, the other at the small of her back. She stopped in the doorway and stooped to pick something up.

"Does this belong to either of you?" She held up an ankle bracelet. Looking down at my own unadorned ankle, I held out my hand to accept the trinket from her. I expressed my gratitude, but was cut off mid-sentence. "You may want to have that looked at. The clasp is loose."

"Thanks again, Angelina. I'll..." But she and Sasha were already gone.

"Well, she was sure in a hurry. And did it seem to you like she was holding something back? She started to say something before she found my ankle bracelet but then seemed to change her mind about it."

"I thought so too," June agreed. "But mostly she seemed to be in a big rush to get Sasha away from us, like she was afraid she was going to tell us something we weren't supposed to know."

I sat down on the sofa, still in thought. "Ouch, what's this?" I reached under my leg and retrieved the object that had been poking me. It was Sasha's locket. "Hmm. I wonder if Sasha left this on purpose. If this is her sister, and she's in trouble, maybe we can figure out where she is. She said someone was holding her on an island."

June took the locket from my outstretched hand and studied the two small photographs. "They look enough alike to be twins, don't you think? As far as being held against her will, that seems a little dramatic. Then again, there are all those rumors about Scorpion Island. After all the research I've been doing, and hearing what Detective Reed told you, I get the feeling there really is something sinister about the place; otherwise, the rumors would have died away. Here, take a look at this report I found in some news archives from last year." She found what she was looking for and handed me her cell phone. I scanned the article and handed back her phone.

"You're right, June. Some of this stuff seems to have a pretty solid basis in facts. You've been busy, haven't you? And here I thought you were sending sappy love texts to Jack this whole time." Her cheeks darkened a shade or two, and she glanced down at the phone. I figured I wasn't completely wrong in my assessment after all.

Chapter Twenty-Eight

What, man, defy the devil. Consider, he's an enemy to
mankind. ~*Twelfth Night*

Even though life kept throwing flaming curve balls at us, we
still had to eat. We chose a small outdoor cafe at the edge
of the marina for a casual supper, where we ordered a light meal
and iced tea. (Shocking I know, but after this afternoon, I felt it
was best to keep a clear head this evening.) We rehashed the
recent events yet again, trying to figure out how to untangle
ourselves from the web of mystery we were snared in. I was
determined to finish off this weekend, not only alive, but
assured that whoever was terrorizing Devil's Island was brought
to justice.

I was about to make a dent in my avocado and tomato
salad when I spotted Angelina coming out of the marina office.
She was carrying a leather satchel and walking like she had
someplace to be. She didn't see us, and I decided now was
not a good time to engage her in a conversation, even though
there were still a number of questions I would have liked her

to answer. She headed for the finger dock directly in front of the office where many of the bigger, luxurious sail boats were berthed. In spite of the fact that I was a powerboat person through-and-through, I couldn't help but admire the graceful lines of the sailing vessels. Angelina stopped about halfway down the dock, in front of a majestic, triple-sailed boat with a jet-black hull. Across the transom, in red letters edged in gold leaf, was the name, Devil Chaser. The last letter of 'Devil' was formed from a stylized scorpion glittering in the sun. She tossed the satchel over the gunnel onto the deck, spun around, and strode back in the direction from which she had come.

"Wouldn't it be nice to just hop on your luxury yacht and sail off to some exotic port whenever the whim struck?"

June cocked her head and gave me a quizzical look. "Umm. Hello. You and Hamm don't have it so bad, you know."

"You're absolutely right, I know. Sometimes, other people's lives just seem so much more glamorous than my own."

"I'd say they have the glamour thing down pat. Isn't that Damien pulling into the parking lot in that way less-than-ordinary Bentley?"

"I can't tell for sure through the tinted windows, but I'm guessing by the license plate it must be him." I couldn't think of anyone else who would drive such a fancy car with MAGIC1 spelled out on its plates.

June looked back at the office then at me. I guessed it must have been the sun's reflection off the water that made her eyes glow like embers. Either that or I was still feeling the effects of my afternoon wine. "It's now or never, Francie. I say we stow away on that sailboat, and see if it's headed where I think it is. I don't think they're planning a long trip with the convention going on, and I only saw that one little duffel bag. Both of them seem like the types who require a much higher level of maintenance than you could fit in that bag. I think your day-to-day purse holds more stuff than what's in there. Now, are you ready to get some answers?"

So much for my resolve to keep my nose out of the mystery and leave the detecting to the detective.

"Um, if I say no, are you going to go anyway?"

"Well, of course."

"I guess I'm in then. I would rather be in the midst of danger with you, than sitting here alone wondering what you got yourself into. Besides, who knows what else I'd get framed for while you were gone. I'm in."

June and I left the remnants of our meal and strolled nonchalantly down the dock toward the beautiful sailboat. We were just two friends enjoying the summer air and admiring the boats bobbing peacefully at their docks. It was a good thing the blinds of the marina office were shut against the evening glare of the sun because I couldn't see into the space and assumed whoever was inside couldn't see out. Nevertheless, I glanced back toward the building more than once, fearing that we'd be spotted. Guilty conscience? Without a doubt. I had just agreed to board the vessel belonging to the two most important people at the resort without permission or even a remotely valid reason.

It took only seconds to hop aboard, step over the leather satchel on the teakwood deck, and slip quietly through the unlocked door to the cabin below. Nothing appeared out of the ordinary unless you counted the impeccable decor. No sooner had I pulled June into a cedar-lined closet in what I assumed was guest lodging and shut the door, than we were rocked to the side and found ourselves surrounded in luxurious-feeling and smelling fabrics. I wished I could see better. I imagined being invited on board and instructed to help myself to anything I needed or wanted. After a few seconds, we heard animated voices above us. Damien and Angelina were both speaking quickly, but from the sounds of their voices, neither of them seemed angry or upset. I held my breath and June's hand while the boat slowly pulled away from its berth, turned and started on its course to destination unknown.

Chapter Twenty-Nine

Have more than you show, speak less than you know. *~King Lear*

Before my legs even had a chance to cramp, I could feel the speed and direction of the boat change. We had slowed down and turned sharply. I couldn't tell the heading because the dark, claustrophobic closet space was playing tricks on my sense of direction. I was glad I had checked the time on my cell phone just as we were leaving our dinner table because now, based on the brass ship's-wheel clock above the mahogany desk, I knew it had been about a twenty-minute boat ride to where we now found ourselves. I'm not that great in math, but figuring the speed of the sailboat to be about ten knots, I calculated that we must be on one of the smaller islands near South Bass, perhaps Middle Bass, or Little Sister. The only other possibility would be Scorpion Island, the place shrouded in rumors and the focus of June's recent intel gathering expedition. I was getting a sinking feeling about this already.

Movement on the deck above us brought me back to the situation at hand. The boat listed to the right, and I felt a bounce and then a second one. Angelina and Damien had stepped off the boat and the sound of their footsteps receded. They had gone ashore.

"Now what, super-spy?" I was getting cranky either because I was mad at myself for agreeing to June's hare-brained scheme or because I didn't have enough time to finish my dinner. I never even got the chance to look at the dessert menu. It was a toss-up.

June headed straight for the nearest porthole and stuck her nose on the glass. "Let's figure out where we are, then we can decide what we should do."

At least I agreed with her on that point. I strode over to the little oval window opposite her and squinted into the sun reflecting off the water. "Nothing here," I noted, cozying over to her spot to get a better look at the view from her window. "Wait, does that guy have a gun?" There was a man off in the distance dressed in some sort of uniform, and as he turned to retrace the straight line he had just walked, it was clear that there was a rifle slung across his back. Just off to his right, we both saw Angelina and Damien at the same time. They walked right past the guard, or whatever he was, nodding in recognition, but not slowing down. He nodded in return and pointed in the direction they were walking, up to the high point of the island. I followed his finger's lead to a large white structure at the top of a hill. It looked like a majestic southern plantation house.

"Hey, June, let me see your cell phone. That building looks like one of the hotels from the Wikipedia article you showed me about Scorpion Island."

June pulled out her phone, but when she tried to access the file, nothing came up. "There's no reception here, Francie. Nada. Not even a single bar." She stopped short. "What the heck? Francie, are you seeing what I'm seeing?"

I forgot about the cell phone and looked out the window once again. "Now what?" Eddie Sneed was driving a black golf cart decorated with a gold-leaf script—the very same script as on the transom of the DeVille's boat. He stopped at the top of the hill next to the guard and handed him something. It looked like a lunch tray. "What in the name of weasel hats is he doing here?"

"It can't be good, whatever it is. Either he's gotten himself into some deep doodoo, or he is one of the bad guys. I'm going to call his cell phone and confront him. I can't believe I actually added him to my contacts at the first meeting we went to. Let's hear him explain his way out of this."

"Or not," I sighed. Picking up her phone from the floor where she dropped it, I reminded her of the absence of signal. "What good is modern technology if you can't rely on it during an emergency?"

"You can still access my contacts list can't you?" June didn't seem as depressed as I was over our total isolation and vulnerability.

"Yes, but..."

"Just find his number. Actually, just pull up the contacts list. We'll be fine."

I didn't question her cryptic order. I just did as she asked. "Okay. So, here it is. Now what?" June pulled a gadget out of her small bag that looked to me like a key drive or bluetooth device. "What's that? I never saw that thing before."

June explained to me that it was a goTenna prototype given to her by a techie upstart company to test out and review in *Tech Times* magazine. She explained to me that it was supposed to work without any wifi or cell towers to send messages and locations in case of a downed power grid. I was impressed. "How convenient."

June laughed as she connected the device to the mic outlet on her phone. "It's time to test this thing out in a real life situation. Come to think of it, I'm surprised you didn't have one of these in your purse. You usually have the 'save-the-day' item rolling around in that bottomless bag of yours."

She was right. I usually did, but not this time. I was glad she pulled the rabbit out of the hat, and watched with interest as she used the magic bunny to send out an SOS signal to anyone who might be in the area with an active GPS location. You couldn't call a specific number, but it was communication. Hopefully it wouldn't backfire and end up giving away our presence to the bad guys.

"Hey MacGyver, there's a phone over here in the salon that looks like one of the satellite phones they always use in TV action shows. Should we give it a try to call Eddie?"

"It can't hurt. Punch in his number, and then hand it over. I have a thing or two to say to that little ferret."

I input Eddie's number into the giant apparatus, giant at least compared to my iPhone, and sure enough, it started ringing. I didn't want to be on this end of the line if Eddie picked up, so I tossed the device to June who treated it like a hot potato, bumbling it all around like it was scorching her fingers. Finally, she put it to her ear. I could hear Eddie's calls of "Hello?" from three feet away.

June took a deep breath and let loose her wrath. "Okay, Sneed. Quit beating around the bush and tell me right this minute what game you're playing. No more spy games, secret meetings, or disappearing acts. Talk!"

For the first time since we met him, Eddie didn't say a word. June held the phone away from her ear for a second and checked the connection to make sure she was still online. I could hear the crackle from the satellite phone but nothing else.

"Listen, Weasel. We know exactly where you are and that you're up to your ears in something shady. Somehow Francie and I keep getting drawn into situations, and you seem to be right in the middle of all the trouble. Now, talk!"

Chapter Thirty

Love all, trust a few, do wrong to none. *~All's Well That Ends Well*

While June continued to give Eddie a piece of her mind, I stepped back over to the porthole with the view so I could get a look at Eddie as he explained his actions. The next time I heard Eddie's voice it didn't sound anything like the ingratiating, overzealous nimwit we had come to know and not love. "Listen, June. This is not a game. This is not a drama exercise. What this is is life and death, and you need to listen carefully."

Even though I was five feet away, I could hear him clearly. But in contrast to his new, commanding voice, he was shifting from foot to foot and looking right to left and over his shoulder, clearly uncomfortable and agitated.

June wasn't buying it. She cut him off before he could say anything else. "Eddie, you little sneak, you better tell us what's really going on, and be quick about it."

Still observing Eddie through my little window, I knew the exact moment he spotted the Devil Chaser. He froze in place and stared right at the boat. I don't know how June was still holding the receiver to her ear because I had no trouble hearing his next questions.

"You're onboard the DeVille's sailboat aren't you? Are you nuts? Do you have a death wish?"

June did not reply. I was wondering who the real Eddie Sneed was. Was he the annoying but harmless interloper from the convention? Or the manipulating force behind the accident at the beach office? Was he a klepto-clown trying to untangle his association with a blackmailer? Or maybe, like us, he had found himself way over his head. Perhaps he was trying to unravel the mysteries and prove himself a worthy sleuth, but instead became another victim of something much bigger and sinister than any of us had imagined.

June covered the mouthpiece of the sat-phone and whispered, "What should I tell him? I think he knows we're on the boat."

Before either of us had a chance to come up with a good response, Eddie's voice got deathly serious. In a low, measured tone, unlike anything we ever expected to come from him, he continued. "June, you and Francie need to stay where you are. I'll figure out a way to get you ashore before you both end up getting killed."

I had to get right next to June and put my ear up to the receiver to hear what he said next.

"Listen to me. It is not safe for you to stay on board that boat. I'm sorry if I'm scaring you, but seriously, you should be afraid, very afraid. Now just stay put. Don't do anything to give away the fact that you're on this island. You do not want these people to know you're here if you ever want to get back to your families and your normal lives." The line went dead. The connection was lost.

"Is he for real? What's going on here?"

June hung up the phone and sat heavily on the nearest chair. "I'm sorry, Francie. This was probably a very bad idea."

"It's too late for that kind of talk," I replied, even though I had to silently agree with her. "Let's focus on what we need to do right now. Do you think he's telling the truth about us being in danger?"

"Well, throughout all of this, I get the feeling that he actually does like us, maybe even a little too much or in a weird sort of way. I'm feeling like we should trust him for now."

I agreed with June and went back to look out the window. June got up and joined me, and we both pressed our noses against the glass to watch Eddie walk back over to the guard. He appeared frantic and gestured wildly in the direction of the main building. The guard looked irritated, but eventually he left his post and started walking up the slope toward the white building at the top of the hill, glancing nervously back at Eddie who was standing in the spot the guard had just vacated, presumably taking over his post for the time being. As soon as the guard was out of sight, Eddie ran straight for the docked sailboat.

"Psst." Eddie called to us in a strangled whisper. "Girls, you can come out now, but lay low and don't say anything for now."

We did as we were told, peeking tentatively out the cabin door. In a calm and reasonable voice that we had never heard from him, he directed us to quickly and quietly follow him.

I stayed right where I was for a moment, scrutinizing Eddie from head to toe. I needed to make one hundred percent sure it really was him before putting my life in his hands. I concluded that it would be nearly impossible to impersonate this five-foot five skinny guy with a bad toupee and a knack for choosing the most horrible wardrobe combinations known to man. And then there were his voice and mannerisms which even the best actor would be hard-pressed to imitate to the degree of accuracy necessary to fool my trained eye. Yep, to the best of my knowledge, it was indeed Mr. Eddie Sneed who now stood before us and was about to give us orders. What other choice did we have? We closed the cabin door and silently followed him off the boat, down the dock, and up a path leading in the opposite direction from the one the guard had taken.

We walked in silence for about a half mile on an overgrown path until Eddie stopped in front of a low, cement-block building very similar in appearance to the dormitories back on Devil's Island where the summer employees resided. Definitely not one of the attractions listed on our all-access V.I.P. passes. To make matters infinitely worse, the ugly building was surrounded by cottonwood trees.

Eddie put his index finger to his lips and brought us around to the back entrance where, about ten feet from the door, a rickety, rusty, metal staircase led up to an equally unsafe-looking balcony that ran the entire length of the second story. Without a word, he gave us a signal to follow him up, and up we went. At least the building didn't have eight stories.

Once on the balcony, if you could call it that, Eddie pulled a key from his pocket, inserted it into the lock on the door leading inside, pulled the door open and slipped inside. Again, we followed.

The room we found ourselves in was cheerless and musty-smelling. Threadbare, dun-colored curtains hung listlessly at the sides of the single, high, grimy window that looked out over the scraggly tops of the cottonwood trees.

I figured it was okay to speak at this point. Standing with my feet firmly planted and my hands on my hips, I cleared my throat and mustered up my best teacher voice. "Eddie, you need to quit stringing us along and explain right now exactly what is going on here." Then I waited.

He looked at me, then over to June whose arms were crossed over her chest. She was waiting too. "All I can say right now is that your snooping is liable to get us all killed. Why did you come here in the first place? It was obvious you weren't all that concerned about my whereabouts or safety."

The guilt trip he was laying on us was working. I remembered being glad that Eddie hadn't shown up at the theater, and angry when we saw him at Bob's house. There was concern for his well-being when he disappeared from the fun house, but the main reason we were here was to find out how he fit into all the weird stuff going on and to get some answers. I was tired of being interrogated by the police in connection to events to which I had no connection other than being in the wrong place at the right time.

There would be no satisfactory explanation from Eddie, at least not yet. What he did was give us more orders. "Stay right here until I come back for you. There's a slim chance I can get you off the island safely. I repeat, stay here. Trying to leave will only end badly. The people here are not open to visitors, especially Nosy Nancies. I'm serious. now promise you'll just stay here. You will stay, won't you? You know I'm trying to help right?"

Eddie was regressing back to his old annoying self. It was comforting in an odd way. He continued his running monologue as he backed away from the center of the room toward the door. Before either June or I realized what was happening, he was pulling the door shut behind him. We stood there, a little shocked, a little embarrassed, realizing when we heard the click-thunk of the lock that he had gotten the better of us.

"Wait a minute," I said as June sprinted to the door, twisting and jangling the knob in a futile attempt to get it to turn. "What kind of dormitory has rooms that lock from the outside?"

"Apparently, this kind," June snapped. I could tell she was angry at herself for being duped by such an unworthy adversary, so I let her curt reply go.

"Focus. We need to focus and prioritize. What is our goal? What are our options?"

"Seriously, Francie? You sound like a life coach, not someone tricked by an oversized rodent and trapped in a cement cell on an island run by criminals."

"We don't know that for a fact. All we know is that Eddie is being his overdramatic self. He probably wants to prove to us that he's a hero and can save the damsels in distress."

"Namely us."

"Well, let's not sit around moaning about it. We need to come up with a way out of here."

"You're right. What about the window? I think I can reach it if I pull that desk chair over."

It didn't take long for June to determine that opening the window wouldn't be an option. The grime on the glass camouflaged a diamond pattern of steel wire embedded between two panes of glass, most likely shatter-proof, at that. From my spot on the narrow bed, it was plain to see there were no other exit options. Other than where June and I sat, the only other furniture in the room was a cheap metal desk and an old wooden dresser with a murky mirror hung above it. The rest of the room's space consisted of a small closet and a windowless bathroom of about the same size. Since it didn't look like we would be leaving on our own any time soon, we decided to look more carefully at the contents of the room. Maybe we could uncover some clues as to who lived here or what kind of a dormitory this was. I started with the bathroom. June took on the dresser and desk. Opening the medicine cabinet, I found a bottle of generic aspirin, some contact lens solution and a lonely tube of lip gloss. Nothing behind the toilet or in the tank, a bar of Ivory soap in the shower. Not even a bottle of shampoo or conditioner. Either the resident was bald, or this was a bare-bones, essentials-only room. Boot camp? Reformatory? Prison? None of these thoughts gave me the least bit of comfort.

June had more area to cover, so she was still busy opening drawers when I stepped back into the room. She glanced over her shoulder at me and nodded toward the bed, "Over there. That's what I've come up with so far."

"Not much, I see. I didn't find anything in the bathroom to indicate whose room this is. No prescriptions, but we do know the occupant wears contact lenses."

"And it's a girl based on the clothes in the drawers. Nothing to give away any sense of her style, although she must be petite. The few things she has are all extra-small. There are a few flashier outfits that look more like costumes in the back of the closet. They're probably from the previous tenant though. They appear to be too big to fit whoever rooms here now."

I sat on the edge of the bed and looked at the pathetic collection of personal belongings June had gathered so far: a pair of tortoise-frame eyeglasses, an employee name tag that looked like the standard-issue ones worn by all the employees at Devil's Island, and a photo in a black, wooden frame. I assumed the glasses were for when our mystery girl wasn't wearing her contacts. The name on the name tag said Sofia, and the picture looked uncannily familiar. Two girls, their arms around each other's tiny waists, smiled brightly for the photographer. I recognized the girl on the left instantly. I'd seen her enough times since our arrival at the convention. The girl on the right was almost a mirror image of Sasha except she looked to be a little younger, had dark hair and piercing green eyes. And now we knew her name was Sofia.

The rest of our search didn't uncover anything more of interest. We didn't find a secret passage in the back of the wardrobe leading to an enchanted world or a keypad with a code to spring the door open. No phone numbers, no address book, just the photo and the name tag.

You never realize how long an hour really is until you are forced to remain in a place with nothing to do except tick off the passing minutes. June and I had exhausted all the possibilities we could think of, and were starting to give in to a sense of resignation regarding whatever might be in store for us, when a rustling on the other side of the door got our attention. Someone fumbled with a key in the lock and then the door creaked open. Before I could think of an appropriate insult to hurl at Eddie, Sasha's sister, Sofia, let out a scream, dropped the bag she was holding, turned and bolted out of the room, down the stairs and away from the building. It must be a genetic thing, or more likely, a response to living in fear. June had the good sense to dive for the door, managing to catch it with her shoulder seconds before it could imprison us for a second time. I scooped up our meager evidence along with June's phone and tossed them all into my handbag before heading out behind my friend.

Chapter Thirty-One

...To rush into the secret house of death,/Ere death dare come to us? *~Antony and Cleopatra*

Now that we were finally outside, we had a few things to figure out. Were we alone? Were we under surveillance? How could we safely get off the island? What was Eddie up to? And finally, what should we do about Sofia?

First things first. "Aah...choo!" That set off a sneezing fit that brought tears to my eyes and a look of horror to June's. When I could finally breathe normally again, the first thing I did was to curse the very existence of cottonwood trees. They were determined to kill me one way or another.

"Well, Francie, you already answered two of our questions."

"Huh?" Sniffle, sniffle.

"Well, first of all, we must be alone because your honking and wheezing would have brought out the cavalry in no time, and second, I doubt there are surveillance cameras out here among the trees. It's pretty isolated from the looks of things—nothing much of interest to keep tabs on other than the dorm building, and the locked doors do a pretty good job of that."

"Well, you're welcome then," I sniffled again, having nothing of substance to use for wiping my poor nose.

"We can't stand around waiting for Eddie to return, especially since we can't even be sure of his intentions. I know you want to trust him, but I'm having a hard time with that idea."

"I don't like it either, but I find it more reassuring than the thought he is somehow involved in illegal activities and trying to draw us into his game. I agree though that we need to take some action. Let's go see if we can get close enough to the big house on the hill to see what's going on."

We stuck to the path for a short time but we didn't want to end up back at the boat dock, so we headed into the brush, trying to keep to the more wooded areas and walking uphill until we got a glimpse of the big white house on the hill. I half expected to see it surrounded by armed guards like you see on TV, but that wasn't the case. Come to think of it, we were on a well-protected private island, inhabited by private club members who probably felt pretty secure against the threat of uninvited trespassers. And yet, here we were.

We kept our distance from the imposing house, and kept ourselves pretty well hidden for the most part thanks to the tall hedge of evergreens surrounding the yard, the wooded area beyond the main grounds, and the fact that dusk had settled in over the island, creating lots of interesting shadows to provide some additional coverage. After circling the property and determining it would be possible to approach it from the side where the garage was located, we decided we needed to get a closer look at who was inside and what, if anything, was going on. Through a low window on the back side, we could see the glow of a light between the slats of window blinds that ended about a half inch shy of the windowsill. We agreed that this would be our destination.

"What do you see? What's going on in there?"

I had to shush June with a finger to my lips. There was only room for one snoop under the window, and this time it was me. I remained very still, even holding my breath, so as not to give our presence away. The room I was looking into was an office or study. Several highly-polished tables were positioned around the room. An olive-complected man with jet-black hair sat at the one closest to the window, a little to my left, concentrating on the task before him. There was a satchel on the table that looked disturbingly like the one Angelina had brought with her onto her sailboat. The man reached in the bag and drew out a stack of neatly-wrapped cash. He laid it down on the table in line with a row of stacked and bundled bills exactly like it.

He paid no attention to the other activities going on around him. At a second table, directly in my line of sight, there were four equally menacing-looking men engrossed in a card game that I was pretty sure was not Old Maid or Go Fish. The third and final table was occupied by a pair of younger men, probably in their thirties, but no less intimidating in their dark suits. These two were looking through a collection of papers that from my vantage point looked like photographs and spec sheets. Six young girls, late teens to early twenties, stood against the wall positioned behind the card-playing group. They did not look happy to be there. They did not speak, and none of the men spoke to them.

June was tugging at the hem of my pants which by now looked nothing like the crisp, summery, white linen slacks I had put on after our spa visit which now seemed like it happened weeks ago. I waved her off, but she was not going to sit idly by while I got all the intel. She tugged again.

When I had committed the scene to memory, I moved away from the window and around the corner. June followed and we both scooted ourselves down onto the grass with our backs up against the windowless garage. "What's going on in there? Did you recognize anyone?"

I recounted everything I saw in detail. June's eyebrows came together as she thought about what I had just told her. "We can't really come to any definite conclusions based on that, but it doesn't sound like they were planning a holiday barbecue. Let's go around to the back of the house and see if we can find out anything else. And this time, you get to be the lookout and I will be the 'look-in.'"

Since we were right up against the house now, it was a little easier to make our way around to the back yard—easier logistically, that is, not physically. I was racking up some major activity points moving around the house in a deep squat. My thighs would be screaming in the morning. When we reached another window with a light on, we made sure we could peek in without being seen and then June had her turn. After a minute, she stepped away from her post. The first things I noticed were her pale face and worried expression. "What did you see, June? Were there more girls in there?"

"Oh yes. There are more girls. Four of them, and they aren't dressed as waitresses or house maids. In fact, they're barely dressed at all."

"What? What do you mean?"

"They were lined up against the wall. There are four men in there too. Three of them looked like they were arguing or bidding on the girls. The fourth man shook one of the other guy's hands then offered him the hand of one of the girls. The slob took her and practically dragged her over to a flight of stairs."

"I don't believe this, June. Move. I want to see for myself." Of course I knew she wouldn't lie to me, but what she was describing was just too awful to be true.

I slumped down beside June, abandoning my post at the window. "I think they are selling girls in there. It looked like the other two men were bidding again, and the winner disappeared upstairs with another one of the girls. The last guy wandered off looking deflated. Ugh. This is disgusting. Do things like this really happen right here, practically in our own backyard?"

"I don't know. Everyone assumes that sex trafficking rings only exist in major cities or third world countries, but if the mob really does occupy this island, then I'm sure nothing is out of the realm of possibility."

I sank even lower to the ground, the weight of what I had probably just witnessed acting like a heavy anchor on my heart. "We have got to find a way off this island so we can tell Detective Reed what's going on. Do you think Bob found out what was going on here and threatened to expose the operation? Do you think that's why he was killed?"

"I don't know, Francie. It's possible, but we can't prove anything, and unless we can sprout wings or grow some gills, how are we going to escape from this island? Do you have any more tricks up your sleeve, or more accurately, in your bag?"

I began rummaging madly through the depths of my handbag, pulling out three different shades of lipgloss, two empty bottles of hand sanitizer, a book of matches from the Cheesecake Factory, and a month-old IOU for a kayak rental. So far nothing looked very promising. Before I could continue my scavenger hunt, a shadow completely blocked out the last anemic ray of sun illuminating our hiding spot. I looked up to locate the source of the unexpected blackout, but before I had the chance to scream, a clammy hand smelling faintly of salami and garlic clamped over my mouth. June was being silenced by Eddie Sneed's other palm.

Chapter Thirty-Two

This is the night. That either makes me or fordoes me quite.
~Othello

The noise of a helicopter's blades whooshing through the clouds sounded like a tornado above the quiet island. Men in black T-shirts and cargo pants, sporting some serious muscle and very menacing weapons, came hurtling out of the house, the woods, and the shadows like ants clamoring to a forgotten piece of watermelon. So much for residents who felt secure against the threat of uninvited trespassers. The armed guards were all focused on the helicopter hovering above their secret island lair.

Eddie removed his hands from our mouths, but the smell of an Italian sub lingered under my nose. "Stay quiet! You couldn't just stay put, could you? I told you I would be back, but no, you had to go out on your own and alert everyone on the island that there has been a breach."

I started to protest, but the minute I opened my mouth, Eddie cut me off and continued berating us. "If I was able to find you two twice on this island without even looking for you, just imagine how easily you will be hunted down by these trained guerrillas. I almost had everything set to get you away from here, but now we're going to have to go to Plan B."

"There's a Plan B?"

Eddie stopped June before she could say anything more. "Do exactly what I say, nothing more, nothing less." Eddie stopped long enough to look into both of our eyes, impressing upon us the utter seriousness of the situation. "Follow the trail that leads through the woods until you reach the old wooden dock on the south edge of the island. A friend will be there waiting for you. Go right now while the guards are distracted, and take this."

"A friend? Seriously?" I had to speak my mind before we just blindly followed Eddie's orders. "Why are you helping us, Sneed? What do you have to gain? You sure seem to be mixed up in all of this, and I have no idea why we should trust you. You might be leading us right into the scorpion's nest. Literally."

"Listen. There's no time to explain everything now. When we're all back safe and sound, I'll tell you all I know. I'm really sorry for causing you so much trouble, but believe me, my hands were tied. I had no choice." Eddie thrust a large sealed envelope into my hands. "Take this to the police as soon as you get back. Now go. Hurry."

He practically pushed us out into the open where we had to stay low and run along the edge of the house until we got to the semi-shelter of the sparse woods and the trail that, according to Eddie, would lead us to our rescue from this insane island. The path, as Eddie had called it, was really just some trampled down weeds with sticks and rocks and small dips and holes threatening to knock us off our feet with every step. It was a test of stability and dexterity keeping to the path while avoiding getting tangled up in vines or twisting an ankle in one of the holes. Night had settled in, and the cover of the trees made it all the more difficult to navigate this unfamiliar terrain. There was only enough room to proceed single-file, so I split my time concentrating on the ground in front of me and turning backward to reach for June's hand, making sure she was right behind me, zigging and zagging all the while to avoid obstacles.

The whirring of the helicopter rotors circling above us provided an appropriate soundtrack for the bizarre movie scene playing in my head. I hoped the noise would continue to occupy the attention of those armed men until we reached our destination and whomever Eddie had contacted to rescue us. I hoped he could be trusted. It was getting harder and harder to tell who was tangled up in this mess and what roles people like Angelina and Damien DeVille played in this crazy drama.

Finally, we stumbled out of the trees into a patch of emerging moonlight. As it turned out, our forward momentum kept us in motion a few beats longer than what would be considered prudent, once we realized that the trail ended abruptly at the edge of a rocky cliff about twelve feet above the water. Twirling our arms like a couple of crazy windmills, June and I ended up stopping just short of cliff diving. "A little warning would have been nice, Sneed," I mumbled to myself.

I sat down hard on the scrubby earth. "What now? Where's our go-to guy?" June got down on her knees beside me and peered over the edge of the rocks. "Be careful, June.

If you tumble headlong off this cliff, I'll be left alone here on this hellacious island to get sold off to the highest bidder or whatever is happening to those poor girls in that house of horrors." I got off my butt and onto my knees so I could hold onto June's ankles. She was getting too close to the edge for my liking.

June stretched herself about as far she could, and I gripped her ankles with everything I had in me. I wasn't about to lose my best friend now. She let out a shout and whipped her head back and forth causing me to scoot forward on my knees. What was left of my white slacks offered a bit of protection to my knees.

"Gunner! Oh, Gunner, you big beautiful angel! What are you doing here?" A familiar furry head with pointy ears and a wagging tongue popped up and licked June's face from chin to cheek. Between gulps of giddy laughter, June found words to greet our four-legged savior. "Gunner! I have never been so happy to have my face nearly licked off. Are you here alone, or did you bring a friend?"

I don't know who I thought Eddie was sending to meet us, but I was relieved when I recognized the German Shepherd who was now standing on the precipice beside us. Our agile furry friend was truly a sight for sore eyes.

"Michael and Gunner must have come to rescue us." I watched as Gunner took up his loving licks and nuzzles all over June's hands. She lowered herself into a deep-knee bend to give him a proper welcome, circling her arms around the big dog's neck. "Look Francie. He has a rope around his neck. Michael must be waiting down by the water."

I had no clue how Eddie knew Michael, but at least now I was reassured that he was, in fact, one of the good guys. I had met Michael and his faithful companion just a month ago, when he helped clear my husband's name in connection to an arson and murder on Kelleys Island. I wasn't surprised then, when he turned up here, on Scorpion Island, where the idea of organized crime and underworld influences was seeming more and more plausible by the minute. Michael was a solitary man, ex-military, with a keen interest in keeping his new island sanctuary free from the insidious talons of unsavory characters. He had a particular knack for uncovering deeply-layered plots against unsuspecting islanders, and he had the resources to make things happen, usually within the parameters of the law.

"This is a long rope, you have here, buddy. I'm guessing it's for us to get down to the beach, so we can leave here." Gunner responded to June's comment with a woof and a dozen or so additional doggie kisses.

"Mama Mia! Rock climbing is not even remotely one of the items on my bucket list. Isn't there an elevator somewhere? Heck, I'll take the stairs. It's not that I'm afraid of heights, it's just that I'd like to survive this weekend."

"Come on Francie. Our options are pretty limited here. In fact, this is probably the only one we have. Help me tie this rope off to one of the trees."

Gunner bowed his head, and the black nylon rope plopped to the ground. There was no doubt in my mind that Gunner knew exactly what we were saying and what his role was. I trusted this dog more than a lot of humans I knew. Before I could finish pondering the possibilities of human versus canine intelligence, June was testing the strength of her recently-executed knot around a sturdy-looking tree near the edge of the cliff. I wanted to check it myself. Having tied my fair share of sailor knots over the years, I knew how to make sure the line was secure and fit for the job at hand. This was not to say I looked forward to the next step in this project. I may have been employing stall tactics if I wanted to be completely honest with myself.

"Let's do this." June sounded like we were about to have some great fun, not throw ourselves over a rocky ledge and shimmy down to the water on the advice of a German Shepherd.

June went first. She maneuvered over the smooth rocks on her stomach and got in position to slide down the rope. Gunner gave me a soulful look over his shoulder. I knew he was trying to reassure me before he and June disappeared out of my sight. That dog should wear a cape, I thought, as I took a deep breath, grabbed onto the rope, and followed them.

Gunner made his way down ahead of me without much trouble. Maybe four legs were better than two, at least for scaling cliffs.

I bumped and scratched my way down the rock wall finding little ledges and footholds to balance myself along the way. My purse, which was slung across my body, bumped heavily against my back where it had migrated during my descent. It felt like it was loaded with bricks. I really needed to clean it out one of these days. As I tucked that thought away in my mental things-to-do file, the envelope Eddie had given me sailed past my line of sight, pages gaily fluttering all around me. I managed to reach the little stretch of sand at the bottom with not much more than a few new scratches and scrapes on my hands and arms. By the time I straightened my back and brushed off my pants, Michael was already helping June into a small, flat-bottomed boat that was rocking gently in the lake. He nodded at me but did not speak, rather he extended his hand and expertly guided me into our little rescue vessel. I recovered as many pages as I could from the cliff-diving envelope that were now scattered along the shore and floating in the shallow water before settling in beside June. Gunner hopped gracefully aboard, and Michael untied the line and shoved off from the shore. Simple as that.

Michael took up the oars and silently piloted our small craft away from the nefarious island until we were far enough away that the sound of the motor would not be heard from shore. Once the craft was under power, Michael spoke for the first time. "I'm glad I received the alert from your goTenna signal, June. I was surprised that you had the device because it's really not something that's made its way into the mainstream consumer population yet. When I got the message from Sneed that the two of you were on the island and needed a way off, I was able to get your location and arrange to meet you on the beach. I give the little guy credit. I had serious doubts about his skills as well as his intentions, but he managed to step up to the task and get the job done."

"What task? What job? I still don't get how he is mixed up in this." I was frustrated by the lack of information being shared with June and me, and I wasn't looking forward to any more implications or questions from the police regarding my involvement in Bob's untimely death, Angelina's accident or the rest of the questionable incidents that took place over the past two days.

Michael did not reply to my question. Instead, he asked one of his own. "Why did you ladies feel it was okay to visit the most highly-protected and heavily-guarded island on the Great Lakes? Don't you realize that you were putting yourself directly into harm's way, and that you were entirely out of your element?"

June and I both remained silent during our chastisement, our faces turning very similar shades of bright pink.

"Did you speak to anyone other than Sneed while you were there? Did anyone besides him see you?"

"We didn't speak to anyone except Eddie." I was beginning to feel the magnitude of our little impromptu stowaway scheme sitting like a lump of damp clay in my stomach.

June's eyes darted over to me, she cleared her throat and added, "There was Sasha's sister, Sofia, too. We didn't exactly speak to her, but she saw us and fled before anyone had a chance to say anything."

I figured it was best to reveal everything we had seen to Michael. He was probably our best bet at sorting through this mess. "I saw Sofia again at the big white house. She was with a group of other girls around her age, and there were shady-looking men with them exchanging money, playing cards, and what looked like bidding on some of the girls."

Michael's expression was stony. "These are potentially very dangerous people. Do you realize how lucky you are? Do Angelina and Damien know you were on board their boat? I hope for your sake, you didn't leave anything behind."

"What do Angelina and Damien have to do with these people?" I asked the question fully expecting to get the silent treatment one more time. "The logo on their boat has the same scorpion we've been seeing everywhere. I noticed several of the men had it tattooed in different places. One guy even had it on his bald head."

"You know," June added, "I just remembered that Bob had a scorpion tattoo on his bicep. There has to be a connection to his death and these guys."

"You ladies are intelligent. You should think carefully, though, before getting yourselves into any more hot water. I'm going to drop you off back at the resort. I suggest you leave the investigation to the police from here on in. I've got some feelers out as well and am doing a little research into some behind-the-scenes stuff. You'll get your answers, but you need to stay out of the limelight for now. Why not sleep on it, and tomorrow keep your eyes and ears open, your mouths shut, and your butts in chairs at whatever workshops you're supposed to be attending." The corner of Michael's lip twitched almost imperceptibly, and there was the tiniest twinkle in his eye. I knew it. The guy did have a heart. As promised, we were deposited back at the resort, right in front of the marina cafe where we so recently ate supper and talked about everything from seminar topics to underworld mob bosses taking over our beloved islands. Moonlight shone on the DeVille's sailboat, Devil Chaser, moored serenely back in her slip, as if all of this had been nothing more than a crazy kaleidoscope of a dream.

Chapter Thirty-Three

O' what may man within him hide, though angel on the outward side! ~*Measure For Measure*

T he night air was wet and heavy. I breathed in the green smell of the lake mixed with the heady scents of popcorn and fried treats from the amusement park as I stepped off our little rescue boat.

I wandered a few feet away from where June and Michael still sat, a line casually looped over a dock cleat, feeling relieved to be back to the relative safety of this familiar island in spite of feeling everything around me was tinted with fifty shades of evil. Looking back toward the boat, the intensity of Michael's gaze upon June while he spoke to her with his large hands on her tiny shoulders, could have heated the summer air for an extra month. I turned my gaze toward the sparkling ferris wheel lording over the park to give them some privacy.

My purse began chirping a text message notification from somewhere deep inside it. I rummaged through all of the very important things I kept close at hand, but rarely really needed, until I found my phone. I was surprised to find it still partially charged since I couldn't remember when I had plugged it in last. It was a message from Angelina.

"You seem to have left something behind on our sailboat. If you don't want me to contact the police, meet me at Bob's cabin in thirty minutes. Bring June."

"Oh no. June, we have a small problem." I looked down at my feet, trying to figure out what we could possibly have left behind from our stowaway excursion. My bare ankle provided the answer. Oh, why couldn't I resist the lure of shiny trinkets with a nautical theme? I turned to the boat slip where June now stood alone with a dazed look on her face. "Snap out of it, I think we are about to be in big trouble." I showed her the text and then sheepishly pointed out my unadorned ankle. I could almost see the wheels turning in June's head, and then she said the words I didn't want to hear.

"We have to meet her Francie. Who knows what kind of story Angelina will tell the police if we don't. We'll be arrested for sure this time. Bob's place is just down the road, so we have a little time to come up with something." The pacing and mumbling to herself commenced as my dear friend went into action plan mode.

The reassuring light of the full moon no longer guided our way. Clouds gathering in the night sky blotted out its beam as we made our way down the unpaved road that led to Bob's cabin. We had come up with a plan, albeit not a very good one on such short notice.

"I can hardly see my hand in front of my face. Are you sure we're going in the right direction, June?"

"Yes, I see a light up ahead. Angelina must be there already. Use the flashlight on your phone to light up this road. I don't want to almost stumble over another cliff's edge."

We stopped walking so I could fish around in my purse for my ever-elusive phone. As I flipped through the screens to find my flashlight app, a dark figure slipped out of the woods just ahead of us. I stifled the urge to scream when I realized that it was Gabriel.

"What are you doing out here, Gabriel? You scared me half to death, maybe even more than half." I had dropped my phone when he appeared, so I was speaking to his knees as I fumbled in the dirt and brush in search of my annoying electronic lifeline.

"Francie, June, you ladies need to come with me. The police have issued a warrant for your arrest, and I think Angelina has lured you out here so the cops can swoop in and take you away. A police surveillance helicopter supposedly spotted you on Scorpion Island, and Detective Reed is convinced that you, Francie, and maybe even June are my brother's killers."

"Whaaat? But we didn't do anything. This is all a big misunderstanding. I'm sure if we talk to the police everything can be sorted out. Don't you think so, June?"

Gabriel interrupted before I could get June's take on the situation. "I wouldn't risk it. The police want this case closed. People are starting to get really crazy about not being able to come and go from the resort, and my brother and Angelina will stop at nothing to get this wrapped up. They are losing money hand over fist with travel shut down. This place is their livelihood, and I wouldn't put it past them to throw you to the wolves in order to get things back up and running. You need to trust me. I've seen how ruthless they can be if their business is threatened. I'm not even sure they weren't the ones behind Bob's murder. He has been a thorn in their side since day one, and they have exhausted every resource trying to get him off of this island."

I recalled Angelina's words to the same effect when we first met her. It felt like the ground was shifting beneath my feet. "I don't know what we're supposed to do. We can't just hide out forever. This is an island, and the police will eventually catch up to us. Won't hiding out like a couple of criminals make us look like a couple of criminals? And it's not like we have any proof of who actually killed Bob. At this point, I'm so confused about who's on what side that I could almost believe I did it. Say something June. What should we do?"

"I'm trying to sort this out. First of all, it wasn't you. I was with you all night, and furthermore, duh. Second, Angelina and Damien do have the most to gain from getting rid of Bob and having his murder pinned on someone else. And finally, whatever role Bob and the goons on Scorpion Island played in this whole creepy stalker thing just doesn't add up. I think we need a little more time to put it all together before we get steamrolled and sent to the slammer for good. Even if orange is the new black, that's one fashion trend I'm willing to skip."

The wind was really starting to pick up. Another summer storm was on its way, and I definitely didn't want to get stuck outside in the rain again.

"Where can we go Gabriel? There can't be many places here that Angelina or Damien wouldn't think to tell the police to look for us."

"I know a place you can stay until I can get to my brother and his wife and talk some sense into them. There's a cabin out on the edge of the island that hasn't been used since the resort was built. It was our family's summer vacation spot when my parents were still alive. Back then, this island was pretty much undeveloped, the construction of the amusement park had just begun, and of course we were pretty excited about the prospect. It was our little slice of paradise. We had the childhood every kid dreams about, at least until the accident." Gabriel became still and silent, staring at nothing.

"What happened, Gabriel?" June approached him and placed her hand tentatively on his forearm. We waited a moment wondering if he would continue his story.

"My parents died in a motorcycle accident. It happened in a construction zone on the freeway during the beginning phases of the amusement park's development." The look on his face was one of inconsolable grief. "I'm so sorry, Gabriel. I had no idea."

"Of course you didn't. Why would you?" I shut my mouth and hoped I hadn't put an end to his sharing.

"The crash was caused by a hazardous roadway condition created by the highway contractor during construction. There were no warning signs alerting motorists of the condition, and there were no construction barrels placed over the hazard to protect motorists. Because of this, my dad encountered the hazard full-on while exiting the freeway and crashed. My mother was thrown from the bike and died instantly. Dad suffered catastrophic injuries that left him paralyzed. The severity of his injuries eventually resulted in his untimely death, but not until five years after the accident. Damien was sixteen when the accident happened, Roberto was fifteen, and I was eleven. My father's lawyer had been actively pursuing a lawsuit against both the construction company and the amusement park from the time of the accident. A wrongful death case in regard to my mother had already been won, and when my father died, the terms of the settlement were doubled. Needless to say, the three of us would never want for money again."

June and I stood huddled under the umbrella of those words for a brief moment. The thought of all that money and security did nothing to keep the sense of pervasive loss from seeping through my skin, sinking deep into my bones.

When Gabriel spoke again, I could hardly meet his eyes. "Damien, being the oldest, decided he wanted to take over the amusement park development and expand the whole operation, turning it into a world-renown destination. He would keep the memory of our parents and the DeVille family alive whatever it took. He became obsessed with the place. He convinced Bob into selling him his share under the condition that he would stay on and manage the marina for as long as he wanted. Bob jumped at the chance. He would have security for life. He had neither the ambition nor the intelligence to manage his own finances and happily embraced his role as black sheep, that is until this week."

"What about you though?" I asked. "You were what? sixteen? when all of this happened."

"I couldn't stand the thought of staying there another day longer than I had to. My money was still in a trust fund, but I agreed to let my brother manage it under the supervision of the family lawyer, retaining my stake in the corporate earnings and receiving dividends. As soon as school let out for the year,

I moved to Chicago to live with my uncle. I've been there ever since."

"So, now Damien is finally rid of the one sore spot in the operation," June ventured. "But what about you? It would benefit him financially if you were out of the picture, wouldn't it?"

"We need to move if we're going to keep you out of harm's way." It was evident Gabriel had revealed as much of his story as he was willing to share for now.

There was a green tinge to the sky and not even a breeze was left to stir the ominous air. It was the calm before the storm.

Chapter Thirty-Four

God has given you one face, and you make yourself another.
~*Hamlet*

Gabriel's car was parked at the marina, so we headed back the way we had come, moving twice as quickly because of the encroaching storm and the fact that we had a guide who knew his way around the entire property in the dark. I slipped into the back seat of the shiny black sports car while June got in the front with Gabriel. After a short distance, he turned from the paved street and drove slowly and confidently down the overgrown lane that led to the outermost edge of the island. Away from the artificial lights of the resort and the glow of the shrouded moon, it was inky dark.

Gabriel pulled into the short driveway of a cottage that would have been considered quaint in its prime. Cedar siding stained gray complemented with blue shutters must have presented a charming fairy tale face to the world at one time. But now, the exterior was chipped and worn by time and neglect, and rough boards were nailed over the windows blinding them from their spectacular views of the great lake. The overgrown yard momentarily illuminated by the car's headlights still hinted at a once carefully-planned and tended landscape.

Gabriel left the car running with us in it and darted around to the back of the cottage. The porch light blinked on, and he appeared at the front door, strode back to the car and snagged his keys from the ignition. Fat raindrops plopped on the windshield. I had been trying to straighten out the damp, crumpled pages from the envelope Eddie had thrust upon me right before we set out to meet our rescuer, but I didn't think there were going to be enough left to be able to make sense of their content when we finally got the opportunity to look at them in the light for more than three seconds. I had the papers in my hand when Gabriel pulled the front seat forward and extended his hand into the back seat to assist me in my exit. A violent gust of wind threatened to slam the door on both of us, but I managed to brace it open with my foot at the expense of losing even more pages from the envelope Eddie had given me earlier.

The sky opened up and rain soaked us as we all ran to the front door of the cottage. Once inside, I leaned against the wall of the small foyer, wheezing from that last burst of intense energy. The reserve was officially empty. I wasn't sure I could even make it past this entry hall into the living room. My hair was plastered over my face, so in between breathing and trying to get my bearings, I pushed the heavy strands away from eyes and took in my surroundings. There wasn't a whole lot to see from where I stood. The faint glow of one dusty table lamp threw a small halo of light in a three foot circle, casting deep, menacing shadows around the rest of the room.

My gaze found its way back to the front door where Gabriel was concentrating on fastening a series of complicated locks. I wondered why so much security was needed for an abandoned cottage and looked to June for an answer. She was right beside me, also facing the front door. She was as white as a ghost, her eyes round as pennies, her hands shaking as she gestured silently at our host. That's when I noticed it. His white button-down shirt was plastered to his skin from the rain, and through the lightweight fabric it was plain to see the intricate scorpion tattoo covering his back from just below his neck to below his, well, I couldn't tell exactly where it ended, but it was clearly a statement impossible to ignore.

Gabriel turned his back on the newly-secured door to see us hanging on to each other's hands and inching away from him and the horrifying evidence that he too was somehow involved in the intricate web of the mysterious scorpion entity. His handsome face contorted into a menacing look that made my skin crawl. How could we have been duped by his heart-wrenching story about family tragedy and believed he wanted to help us. The truth had to be staring us in the face the entire time. "I see you noticed my family's crest."

"What do you mean your family?" Although I was boiling with anger on the inside, my voice came out crackly and squeaky. Nevertheless, I continued. "Isn't the story you just told us about your parents true?"

"The Scorpione family of Chicago is my true family. They took me in after my own parents got themselves killed on that stupid motorcycle. I mean, what kind of responsible parents go flitting around on a two-wheeled death trap? I didn't want to hang around Ohio and be harassed by all the phony friends wanting me to finance their worthless schemes. As soon as I could leave, I did. That part was true. My brothers were old enough to be on their own and didn't much care if I went to live with our uncle in Chicago. We were separated by choice, and we each found our own way to deal with our misfortune."

June had a thing or two of her own to say to the stranger who stood before us. "It doesn't exactly sound to me like you were wallowing in grief, just millions of dollars."

"You have no idea what it was like. My brothers didn't want a punk teenager hanging around, spoiling their grandiose plans. Uncle John thought I was needy and rebellious so he had no objections when I started hanging around Joey Scorpione shortly after I went to live with him. Joey introduced me to a world where forgotten kids like me and my street friend Senora could belong and even take on the world."

"Oh, I'm sure they were more than happy to welcome you and your millions with open arms. What made you think they were any different from the people back home who wanted to take advantage of you and your trust fund?"

"That's exactly it. The money was in a trust fund. I couldn't access it at will even if I wanted to. And besides, no one knew about the money except for my uncle, and he wasn't spreading the words to strangers. He was biding his time, waiting for his own chance to dip his paws in the honey pot."

"Whoa. back the train up!" It took me an extra beat to register what Gabriel had said a moment ago. "Did you say Senora? As in the crazy woman who tried to kill us last month?"

"Yes, Francesca, Nora is my Scorpione sister. I'm sure you noticed her tattoo. The way she dressed, it was pretty much impossible not to. I told her she should've gotten it in a more discreet place, but she's always loved to be the center of attention. She knew she was beautiful and she knew how to work a crowd."

"Well, she wasn't as smart as she thought she was," June interjected, "and I doubt her outfits have been showing off her tattoo to its best advantage in her new digs."

Gabriel waved his hand as if to dismiss us. "I heard all about your meddling in her business when I visited her in the penitentiary before I came out here. She hasn't forgotten either of you to say the least. Imagine my surprise when I recognized your names on the convention registration list."

I wiped my sweaty palms on my formerly-white, formerly-clean linen trousers. My lips were dry and cracked in spite of the tubes of lip gloss still tucked in my handbag. My voice had been reduced to a raspy whisper. "This can not be happening again. What do you want from us? Are you trying to frame us to avenge Senora?"

"It's nothing so diabolical really ladies. Senora got what she deserved in the end. She had no one to blame but herself. I had my own plan that didn't involve her in any way, but it was still kind of sad to see her sitting in that cell wearing an ugly orange jumpsuit."

He didn't look very sad to me. Before I could fully imagine the scene between Gabriel and his former gang girlfriend, or whatever she was, he continued.

"I had always intended to eliminate my dear brother Roberto—let's face it, he was nothing but a thorn in everyone's side. He had all that money and was too lazy to do anything with it. The only thing he spent it on was expensive cameras and high-powered surveillance equipment. Damien was actually worried about the little perv after Angelina found that box of souvenirs in his house in the spring. No one did anything about it though. That was Bob's ace in the hole. He got to live out his pathetic little life, spying on people all over the resort and grabbing every opportunity to blackmail anyone who didn't want their secrets exposed, and believe me, there was no shortage. As long as he didn't interfere with the business, no one really cared how he occupied his time. It worked out for me too. My only regret is that I didn't get to see your faces when you watched the video from those pathetic clowns. Bob was blackmailing them of course, and when the little thieves got wind of your meddling in his murder investigation, they thought they could use you to find and destroy the evidence of their stupid operation once and for all. I just went with the flow. It kept the spotlight far away from me which is just the way I wanted it.

June hadn't said a word in a long time. I couldn't tell what was going on in her head, but I sure hoped she had a plan. I had nothing.

"As for Damien, he was getting a little too wrapped up in the resort and was becoming a threat to my Chicago family's plans to move forward with Devil's Island. The easy answer was to pin Bob's death on Damien, and take him out of the picture. His assets would be frozen while he got free room and board courtesy of the state, but that wouldn't make much difference. We didn't need his funding, just carte blanche control of the resort and all its operations."

I couldn't believe what I was hearing or seeing. The gracious host of our convention was nowhere to be seen. The man who was now frantically pacing and alternately wringing his hands and clasping them behind his back was scaring me. If he could coldly murder his own brother and then set up his other brother to take the blame, what else could he do? What plans did he have for June and me? The only thing I could think of was to keep him talking. I think June had come to the same conclusion.

"How does your unholy plan include Francie and me? We just came to the island for some entertainment and a little education."

"You've gotten an education, don't you agree? You've learned much more than you need to know, as far as I'm concerned. I guess I'd have to call you overachievers. Unfortunately, you two kept getting in the way and taking the suspicion away from Damien. I wouldn't really care if Francie, or both you, for that matter, got arrested, but it's really Damien I want out of the picture. I have a little soft spot for him; at least he's smart and ambitious, not a waste of space like Bob, so I didn't want him dead, just out of my way. It's taken a little bit of extra planning, but things should work out in the end, and I can't say that I'm not just a little bit pleased to get the two of you out of the way for good. I think it will be a fitting birthday gift for my dear Nora. Her birthday is on the Fourth of July, you know."

I had to hold June's hand tightly. She was vibrating and snarling like a lioness protecting her cubs. And then she roared, right in Gabriel's face.

"You will not get away with this. You're going to be arrested and locked up along with your precious psychotic 'sister.' And what kind of insane family member goes around killing his real brothers for a plot of land?"

Gabriel ignored her scathing reproof and proceeded unlocking the door he had so recently secured. "Enough about me and my family. I'm going to go take care of business now that I know you two won't get in my way."

He gestured to the crumpled, water-stained pages I had been holding onto like a lifeline during his rant. "Maybe you'll have enough time to put your amateur sleuthing skills to use to figure out my ultimate plan before my friend Eddie gets here to tidy up loose ends and remove you from the equation once and for all. Senora told me of your fondness for the deep waters of this lake, and I passed the information on to him."

With that last barb, he left us, slamming the door and locking it from the outside. We were left to wait for that rat Eddie and forced to ponder the anticipation of another midnight swim in our beloved Lake Erie.

Chapter Thirty-Five

Thou art a traitor, false to thy gods, thy brother and thy father.
~King Lear

"Give me those papers, Francie. We need to try to figure out what we're up against this time. I recognize the name Scorpione. They're the most ruthless crime family in Chicago. They make most of their money dealing in smuggled and counterfeit merchandise. Lately, they've been branching out into casinos. Don't you remember they were brought up in Senora's trial? The prosecutor was trying to tie her to the family, but she wouldn't say a word against them and took full responsibility, or credit as she called it, for her crimes."

I felt the enormity of the situation piling up and crushing the air from my chest like boulders. I handed June the mangled papers and fell onto the sheet-covered sofa in the center of the little living area. Dust billowed around my head. After a sneezing fit, I closed my eyes and practiced holding my breath for our promised late night swim. At least the water temperature had gone up since May. What was I thinking? I was not going to take this lying down. I sprung to my feet and started doing circles around the room. There was no TV to distract me on my circuit this time, in fact, the only other furniture in the room was a ratty, old end table and a lamp the color of the mud in the driveway. Whoever used this place obviously did not watch HGTV.

"I knew that weasel Eddie couldn't be trusted," I mumbled mostly to myself because June was consumed with the lump of soggy papers. She held the pages close to the lamp, trying to organize them into some kind of order that might help figure out a way to save ourselves and even Damien and Angelina from Gabriel's rotten scheme.

"Aha!" June pumped her fist in the air like she had just scored a game-winning run.

"What did you find? I hope it's instructions on how to crush a disgusting bug named Eddie Sneed. Before I could reach over to give her a high-five, the celebration was cut short by the sound of someone twisting the knob on the front door. "Uh-oh. I think he's here."

I glanced at the door which had gone silent. Maybe it was just the wind from the storm. June looked too, but then ignoring the door, held the pages out toward me.

"It's a casino, Francie. There are pieces of plans here, names of contractors, copies of emails, even some incomplete invoices. You can plainly see Gabriel DeVille's name on several of the documents and some other names you'd recognize from the news, including Scorpione. Gabriel and the Scorpiones want to turn the island from a high-end resort and amusement park to a flashy casino for high rollers with everything from gaming and bars to strip clubs. Those girls we saw on Scorpion Island must have been there for training to be either card dealers or waitresses or dancers."

"That's not quite as terrifying as being sold to the highest bidder, but I doubt that any of them signed up for those jobs when they applied for their work visas and came to Lake Erie for the summer." Sounds were coming from outside the door once again. The handle jiggled and I could hear faint whispering.

"Get over here June. Give me the papers and I'll put them in the zip pocket of my purse. I think Eddie and probably some of the Scorpiones' other tattooed goons are about to take us out for a moonlight boat ride."

June handed me the papers. Her hands were trembling with anger and I'm sure a good dose of fear. "I'm not going. No way we're going to end up on the bottom of the lake. Been there; done that."

Of course I felt the same way. I braced myself against the door with all my weight, knowing full well that one shove from the other side would send me sailing across the floor, but I had to do something. I felt the door being nudged open against my body and then all hell broke loose. The door flew open banging against the wall. The wind howled in, and cold rain shot sideways at me knocking me down like a blast from a fire hose. I flew onto the floor and ended up tangled in a pile of flailing arms and legs and girly shrieking.

I wasn't sure how many of us there were, but there were certainly more than just June and me. Someone had gotten loose. I could hear thumping and bumping in the shadowy room. Since I couldn't get free, I shut my eyes, braced myself and prepared for the worst. Insane kidnappers seemed to be quite fond of conking people over the head when situations got out of control. I waited. Nothing happened. I opened my eyes a crack and saw that the table lamp was on, but it was no longer on the table. June had it raised at shoulder height like a baseball bat, the extra-long extension cord swaying crazily as she shifted her position left to right and right to left. The shade was missing. The bare bulb at the end of the stick lit up the dingy room and cast wild shadows over the walls and floor.

I squirmed my way out from under the weight of the tangled bodies and recognized Eddie Sneed lying on the floor moaning softly. By the time I pulled myself up to a standing position, the last set of arms and legs extricated themselves from the tangle. They belonged to the ubiquitous Sasha. She remained on the floor, cradling Eddie's head in her lap and stroking his head, or was that a cat? By now you'd think I wouldn't be startled every time I laid my eyes on that ridiculous head pet of his. I had to hold back the urge to kick him while he was down, content in the realization that June must have used Eddie's head for a softball. She was still holding the Louisville Slugger lamp at the ready, presumably in case the weasel tried any funny business. Thank goodness for the extension cord. I thought it was odd at first, but since there was only one lamp in the room, I supposed it made sense. I joined June on the opposite side of the dusty old couch—the only thing separating us from Eddie and Sasha.

Even through the gloom of the house, I could see Sasha's eyes were rimmed in deep purple circles, the kind caused from worry, stress and exhaustion, not the latest fashion color trends. I could also see fear and concern in her eyes as she trained them on my own.

Her heavily accented voice broke the silence. She didn't even bother to enunciate in the Midwestern dialect all the European workers were trained in. "Vhy did you heet my Eddie? Ve come here to save you, but you hurt heem."

June took a tentative step forward, extending her arm so more of the lamplight shone on Sasha's face. "What do you mean save us? I think your English needs some work. Eddie was here to kill us. And seeing that you're with him, I assume you were in on the plan to murder us all along. It makes sense now the way you kept mysteriously popping up everywhere we went."

"No. Is not ze truth." Sasha's comment was punctuated by a moan coming from Eddie who was struggling to sit up.

"Come on June. I think we need to get out of here while we have the chance. Who knows how many more of the Scorpiones' henchmen are on their way. I think I'd rather take my chances trying to clear my name from inside the safety of a jail cell than trying to figure out who we can trust in this nightmare."

Eddie wobbled to his feet, setting my fight or flight mode to flight. "We need to go now."

"Hold on Francie, ugh, my head. Why did you hit me, June?"

"What do you mean, why? You were coming here to kill us. Your 'brother' Gabriel told us so." The lamp-bat was once again poised on June's shoulder.

"Could you just calm down and listen for a minute. It's not what you think."

A spark of bravery tingled through me. In all of the fuss, I realized that I'd not seen any sort of weapon. Neither Eddie nor Sasha were pointing guns or knives at us, and she seemed genuinely concerned about the purple, egg-sized bump that had formed above his left eye. Instead of bolting out the open front door, I crossed my arms over my chest, planted my feet firmly on the floor and looked directly at Eddie. "Seriously? How many times do you think we're going to patiently listen to your lame explanations, do as you say, and then wait to be kidnapped or killed? Make it quick. You've got three minutes until we're out of here. As you can see, June is twitching to break her home run record."

Chapter Thirty-Six

Most dangerous is that temptation that doth goad us on to sin
in loving virtue.
~*Measure for Measure*

Eddie rubbed the knot on the front of his head, looked warily at June, and began. "I was on a roll from January until April. I could do no wrong at the Hollywood Casino. Everything I touched turned into gold. They even gave me a key to my own private suite at the hotel and a credit card with no limit."

I was tempted to ask him why he didn't high-tail it to the nearest toupee shop and have them perform an emergency squirrel-ectomy, but I held my tongue, content to shoot him an evil-eye, and let him continue.

"I was living like a regular high roller until about mid-April, and then everything just dried up. I went from blackjack to poker to craps to roulette. I even resorted to slot machines. Nothing worked. It was over and I was broke. That's when the Scorpione family entered the picture. They offered to help me get me out of debt, and even come out ahead. What an idiot I was for listening to them."

He got no argument from me. "So, what was the catch? There's always a catch."

"I had to agree to come to Devil's Island Resort and keep my eyes and ears open, to watch the people around Gabriel and report back on anyone or anything that might hamper the plans he had for acquiring the resort."

"Including killing his own brother?" June's comment sounded like venom.

"I had no idea it was going to go that far. But I was in and I couldn't get out. After I met you two, I tried really hard to come up with a way to get myself out of this mess. I didn't want anything bad to happen to you. I knew these guys would stop at nothing to get what they wanted."

Sasha was holding Eddie's hand, rubbing his palm with her fingers. "What about her?" I asked, nodding at Sasha. "What's her deal?"

They looked at one another and then at us. Then, in stereo, I heard, "We're in love."

That was the last thing I expected to hear. I was sure it was a heartbreakingly romantic tale of forbidden love and equally sure that I did not have the time nor the stomach to hear any of the details. I was right about the forbidden part. As Eddie explained, when Gabriel got wind of the budding relationship, he came up with a clever solution to the problem. Instead of separating them, he relocated Sasha's younger sister, Sofia, to Scorpion Island. By cutting off contact between the sisters, and keeping Sasha so busy working she didn't even have time to sleep, he could be sure all three of them would cooperate under threat that harm would come to the loved one of whomever broke any of the imposed rules. I had flashbacks to the Cheesecake Factory and the spa, and remembering the frightened look on Sasha's exhausted face, believed the whole story.

June lowered her arm. By now her muscles had to be getting sore, and neither Eddie nor Sasha seemed to be any real imminent threat. "Okay, fine. Let's say we believe you. I still don't get how you know Michael. I'm pretty sure you two don't run in the same social circles."

I knew from my brief dealings with Michael at the end of May and our more recent encounter that June was right. She had known him longer, but he was still a mystery man. I knew he was ex-military and that he was vigilant about keeping his little slice of paradise out of harm's way. I knew he had connections. I knew I probably didn't want to know much more than that.

"Michael found me and offered me a way out of my predicament. He would help Sasha and me get out from under the family's control and reunite her with Sofia if I would help him gather evidence against the Scorpione family."

I translated this last bit of information to mean Michael saw Eddie as the weakest link and therefore the easiest to manipulate. If he could only keep track of what he was supposed to be doing for whom, it might actually work. I thought of the papers he had entrusted to me with the sketchy bits and pieces of incriminating information, and his explanation was sounding plausible once again.

"What do you suggest we do now? If all you say is true, we can't just sit here and wait for Gabriel and his goons to come back for us. I'm surprised they're not here already."

June nodded in agreement. "For once, the summer storm is working to our advantage. Do you have any tricks up your sleeve, Eddie? There doesn't seem to be anyplace we can safely go to avoid being found and starting this nightmare over one more time."

Something had been niggling away in the far corners of my mind since I first untangled myself from our visiting lovebirds. "How did you two get here, anyway? I never heard a car pull up, and this place isn't in walking distance to any place resembling civilization."

This time it was Sasha who answered. "Ve drive our Vespa."

"Huh?" I wasn't sure I was getting her drift.

Eddie piped in. "Our motor scooters. Certain island employees are issued scooters if they work in a variety of locations throughout the resort. With all the racket from the wind, you wouldn't have heard us pull up the drive; besides, we stashed them down by the road behind some trees. We each can take on one passenger. I think the safest place to camp out for the night is at Bob's house. We know he won't be returning, and it's the last place Gabriel would think to look for you now."

"Bob's house? Are you kidding me?" The thought made me shiver.

"Can you think of a better plan?"

Chapter Thirty-Seven

The time is out of joint—O cursèd spite,/That ever I was born to set it right!/ Nay, come, let's go together. *~Hamlet*

June paused less than a second then grabbed Sasha's hand. "Let's get this over with. I'm with you." For my best friend, she certainly wasn't giving me a choice in the election of my personal escort. I'd have to keep my eyes squeezed shut and hope I wasn't attacked by a flying squirrel.

We arrived at Bob's cozy cottage in the woods in less than ten minutes, and with utter gratitude I noted the squirrel was still perched serenely atop Eddie's head. The rain had turned into a fine, steady mist and the wind was gone. In its place gathered an eerie swirling fog.

After stashing the scooters behind the house, we entered through the kitchen, the same way June and I had gone in on our prior visit. From the archway leading into the living room, I could see a long furry tail swaying from the armrest of the ugly plaid couch. Michael was waiting for us.

Michael sat beside Gunner, his right foot resting casually on his left knee. He absently stroked the fur between his dog's eyes. They both looked so relaxed and content that for a moment I could almost believe we were stopping by the summer retreat of a close friend for a visit and a glass of wine. But of course, that moment didn't last. Two chairs, equally ugly, were positioned across from the couch. Eddie and Sasha made themselves comfortable. June sat on the couch next to Michael (uh-oh), and I was left standing awkwardly in the middle of the room.

"Um. Is there any coffee in this place? I could use a cup of coffee about now. Or a stiff drink."

"There's coffee in the cupboard next to the sink; cups are in there too. The coffee maker is on the counter, or if you'd rather, there's this." Michael reached down and picked up a dark bottle with a black label I hadn't noticed. "You'll still have to use the coffee cups. There's a wine key in the utility drawer."

I got to work gathering cups and pouring the wine. From my position at the kitchen table, I could see everyone in the living room, hear the conversation, and not feel like an uninvited fifth wheel. June had tucked her feet up on the couch and absently stroked Gunner's fur, managing to look like she lived here. I pulled the one kitchen chair into the room, passed out the mugs of wine, and joined the circle.

Once we were all settled and had sipped our drinks, Michael pulled something out of the pocket of his denim jacket. It looked like a miniature CD or DVD. "While I was waiting for you, I did a little investigating." (As it seems, he was perfectly certain we would end up there sooner or later.)

"Bob had digital cameras strategically arranged around his entire property, both outside and inside this house. I was at the marina earlier today and found other recording devices attached to the building and even a few on some of the docks. They're pretty sophisticated. Either he was smarter than most everyone thought, or he had someone he trusted who installed and maintained the equipment. In any event, he was still a manipulating petty crook with his own agenda for gaining and keeping control of his piece of the resort pie. He also seems to have had a sick fascination with clowns."

June's face turned red. I took a big sip from my mug remembering the photos we had found in this very room. Bob had immortalized more clowns than I ever cared to meet and other personal encounters between resort employees, all fraught with damaging implications. "Thankfully, his obsessive hobbies will not hurt anyone else, and the fact that he recorded nearly everything that happened around him may provide the hard evidence the police will need to convict his murderer and clear the names of the innocent."

"Have you watched the video feed?" I asked the question everyone else in the room was thinking.

"I saw enough to know it was without a doubt Gabriel DeVille who murdered his brother. He stuffed his body into a large blue duffle bag and hauled it away in the trunk of his fancy car. I'm sure there will be plenty of forensic evidence to link him to the crime and put him away for the rest of his life."

"I stumbled over that bag the first night we stayed here. Obviously, Gabriel couldn't have been trying to frame Francie then. He hadn't even met us yet."

Michael sighed. "You two have a way of turning up in all the wrong places."

"It's true then," I added, "Gabriel wanted it to look like his brother, Damien, was responsible, so the resort would have been entirely his and he could move forward with his casino plans. It should become obvious what happened, as soon as the authorities see the proof."

Feeling a bit more relaxed by the knowledge we now possessed, the soothing sips of wine, and the presence of two worthy bodyguards, we agreed to try to get a few hours sleep. Michael would formulate a plan to keep us safe from Gabriel, who having nothing to lose, would be more determined than ever to get rid of June and me once and for all.

Chapter Thirty-Eight

When we mean to build, We first survey the plot, then draw the model. *~King Henry IV*

We woke to the tantalizing smells of brewing coffee and frying bacon. June and I wandered into the kitchen dressed in oversized tee shirts and boxers which someone had conveniently left in unopened packages on top of the dresser in the small bedroom we shared last night. It felt wonderful to be out of my torn dirty clothes from yesterday, but there was still the matter of a shower. Hunger and coffee deprivation trumped stinky at the moment. The table was set with three plates and two mugs. Michael was pouring himself a cup as he flipped bacon in a skillet.

"Are the lovebirds sleeping in?" I asked no one in particular, not caring about the answer. What I really wanted to know was how long before that delicious meat would make its way to my plate. I poured myself a steaming mug and sat down to wait. June did the same.

She looked around the small room and made note of the obvious. "Eddie and Sasha aren't here, are they, Michael. Should we be worried?"

"No, June, it's all part of the plan. Francie, I'm sorry. They had to take your handbag and a few of your personal belongings over to the hotel. You needed to get some sleep, so after we came up with the plan, I had to make a judgement call."

"What plan? What's my stuff got to do with anything?"

Michael walked over from the stove and slid six strips of perfectly cooked bacon onto my plate. "Eddie is taking your bag, along with your driver's licence and a few of your credit cards back to Gabriel, in the hope of convincing him that he finished the job he was commissioned to do last night. Your phone is on the coffee table in the living room with the rest of the contents. You had some interesting stuff in there."

My friend jumped to my defense. "Don't tease her. You have no idea how many times that stuff has come in handy."

"No problem. Sasha and Eddie are staying at the hotel today to keep tabs on Gabriel. Today's the last day of the conference, and Gabriel is going to need to maintain his presence throughout the day. Apparently you two were supposed to help him prepare for the final event of the evening. Since you won't be there, Eddie and Sasha will fill in. I understand he had already volunteered to help out before all this started. That works to our advantage. Gabriel shouldn't suspect anything, and Eddie can keep an eye on him and his actions."

Hard to believe, but so far things appeared to be working out. "So what about us? What are we supposed to do all day? We can't very well show up to any of the workshops."

"And what about Sofia? Michael, you are going to help us get her off Scorpion Island and reunite her with Sasha aren't you?"

"Yes, June, and here's where things get a little tricky. The good news is that none of the players or their bodyguards are aware of your visit yesterday. I would have heard by now. I think the only person besides Eddie and myself who knows you were there is Sofia, and she's the one we need to locate and bring back."

"Are you taking us for another boat ride?"

"What are we supposed to wear?"

"I need a shower!"

"And more bacon."

"Coffee!!"

I thought Michael would need to be treated for whiplash. "Whoa. One thing at a time. I think we better start with the coffee."

June and I lifted our mugs and Michael got up and poured. He lingered a split second behind June, his eyes scanning every detail of her petite frame like a copy machine.

"It's already getting pretty hot around here. I think I'll go shower now. Are there towels?" The thought of using anything belonging to the late Roberto DeVille gave me the creeps, but I couldn't very well complain.

"I anticipated some of this last night, so on my way over I picked up some basic toiletries. There are fresh towels, toothbrushes, soap, and shampoo in the bathroom. Help yourself. While you two get cleaned up, (Did he just wrinkle his nose?) I'll go pick up some things. What size shoes do you wear?"

"There's nothing open at this hour," June countered, "not even the tourist traps."

Michael shot her a "don't ask" look and left through the back door.

"All right then. I'll tidy up in here while you shower. I trust Michael to get us over to the island, but what we need to come up with is how to smuggle Sofia back."

"This whole thing revolves around a casino operation, right?"

"Yeah, so?"

"I may have an idea." I smiled over my shoulder as I made my way down the short hallway to the bathroom.

It didn't take me long to wash the remnants of yesterday's misadventures down the drain. While June got cleaned up, I sat on the couch, my hair wrapped in a towel, a notepad and pencil from among the leftover contents of my handbag in my hands, and a scheme solidifying in my head. I jotted down some final thoughts as June emerged from the bathroom, feeling confident for the first time in a while. This should work.

Chapter Thirty-Nine

Boldness be my friend. *~Cymbeline*

The boat ride over to Scorpion Island was uneventful. The misty morning air even provided us with an extra element of concealment, and that combined with the knowledge that our skipper was a trained professional (in something scary and important), boosted our morale and fueled our determination to get this job done.

We had discussed my plan on the way over, and I was elated that Michael approved, for the most part, the scenario I had laid out. June added a few ideas, and Michael cautioned us to be alert and careful. With his blessings and the assurance he would be waiting for us to take us back to the resort before the final convention dinner, we stepped ashore wearing our new, perfectly-fitting cross-trainers.

First stop, Sofia's dorm room. With the lay of the land still fresh in our minds, we were able to get to the cinder-block structure housing the workers with little difficulty. Knowing that Michael wasn't too far away and having an idea of what we were going to do when we got there, went a long way toward making us feel like we would be successful in our mission. It was a comfort remembering the guards focused most of their attention on the main house rather than the dormitories, but we still used all the caution we could muster to arrive unnoticed. The doors to the employees' rooms locked only from the outside, so we knocked softly, turned the knob, then entered Sofia's room when there was no answer. It didn't take long to go through the tiny space for a second time and retrieve what we needed.

We had to take turns squeezing inside the tiny bathroom so we could get a look at our handiwork. I was thankful I could only glimpse my somewhat cloudy reflection in the over-the-sink mirror from the waist up, making it a little easier to face the fact that I was no longer a twenty-something show-stopper.

"Why do you get to wear the one-piece outfit? I would have doubled my crunches if I knew I was going to be running around with my stomach showing for all to see."

"Because, Francie, you're the one who's spent the last ten years watching YouTube videos on card dealing in your spare time so you could increase Hamm's odds of winning at the blackjack table when you go to Vegas every winter. You've practically made card sharking a second job so you can reap the rewards of his winnings at the Forum Shops at Caesars Palace."

"Well, there is that."

"Besides, I wouldn't exactly call this a dress. I think my backside is showing."

I gave June the once over. She looked pretty good in the shiny gold scrap of a dress. True, it barely covered her bottom and left her entire back exposed, but she pulled it off, especially with her new hair-do. I, on the other hand, felt like an escapee from an Alice In Wonderland nightmare. The Queen of Hearts would just adore my black bra top covered in red and black hearts and equally mortifying miniskirt decorated in hearts, spades, diamonds, and clubs, not to mention the headband with two cards sticking up like the ears of a playboy bunny.

"We better get moving if we're going to find Sofia and stop Devil's Island from being taken over by these creeps. I hope the seams on this outfit hold up. Just keep practicing your Russian accent. We don't want to sound like Natasha from Rocky and Bullwinkle if we have to talk to someone."

I would have to trust our unseen partners to retrieve my handbag and other personal belongings we had to leave in Sofia's room. We had to walk slowly as we made our way up the hill toward the main house. The walk was more difficult than the last time seeing as we were now wearing the high heels that went with our new digs. Of course, we knew we couldn't escape being seen eventually, but I wasn't looking forward to it. I channeled my inner actress as we passed a group of young men being ordered around by a rough-looking armed guard. Telling myself I was performing a role in a play kept me from thinking about the real-life danger we were walking right into. The scene we approached was surreal as the boys dressed all in black took turns aiming their weapons at a target about fifty feet away on the meticulously manicured lawn just in front of the pristine white house. It looked like they were being trained in using high-powered firearms.

Two men with rifles, and who-knew-what other weapons hidden in the cargo pockets of their uniforms, came to attention as we approached the entrance to the house with artificial confidence. It was showtime. The two men stood, unsmiling, side-by-side, blocking the door with arms crossed, taking in our appearance, scanning us from head to toe. It was impossible to miss the intricate scorpion tattooed on the first guard's bulging forearm.

"ID cards," the second guard demanded when we reached the top of the third step. The scorpion on the side of his neck seemed eerily alive as it rippled over the veins in his neck when he spoke.

"Um." So much for my earlier confidence in our plan. "Gabriel sent us." My voice sounded completely unfamiliar to me. My parched throat and fake accent sounded like one of the Babushkas, the old Russian women my grandmother warned me to avoid when she took me for trips down to the Old World Bakery for tea cakes during my visits to her as a young girl.

Neck Tattoo spoke again. "Gabriel did not inform us of anyone new arriving today."

I cleared my throat noisily and spoke quickly, praying to Saint Vitus, patron saint of actors, that our cover wouldn't be blown. "Ve are here to help ze girls. Gabriel thinks our experience vill be good to help train zem. And some are homesick so ve vill be like zere mozhers. He says they vill vork better this way." I was getting into my role, forgetting the grave reality and concentrating on the performance.

"I see. You are card girls' mother," and looking over to June, maybe a beat longer than his boss would approve, "and you are dancing girls' mother?"

"Yes, exactly." Was he actually buying our story?

Begrudgingly, he let us through the front door. A third guard was waiting for us inside. His scorpion tattoo wrapped around his wrist, realistic-looking blood dripping from the creature's poisonous pincers. I winced when he took my elbow to point us in the right direction. "In here, mother. The dealer's table is in here."

"Fine. Zank you. You may go now." I was really feeling this Russian mamma bear thing." The guy wasn't quite willing to leave me on my own apparently. He walked over to the far wall, leaned against it, and crossed his arms. it didn't look like he was planning to go anywhere any time soon.

I picked up a deck of cards and inspected the design on the back. I must say, I was getting tired of seeing these scorpions on everything. Giving June a nod, I dove right into a full-blown demonstration of amazing card shuffling, and dealing. The guard wasn't bored anymore. He leaned forward then inched closer to watch, and finally walked right up to the table leaving his rifle propped against the wall. As soon as he had joined the three young girls watching my every move, June noiselessly slipped out the door. I hoped I could keep them mesmerized by my amazing skills long enough for her to locate Sofia and get her out of the house.

Loud exotic music emanated from a room right across the hall. A female voice barked instructions to a group of about twenty beautiful women dressed in a variety of revealing costumes and scorpion logo apparel. As June joined the students, the instructor gave her no more than a cursory glance, most likely for arriving late, but as long as no one looked too closely, she wouldn't be discovered as having about twenty years on most of them. The pole dancing lessons I gave her for her last birthday were paying off. She blended right in and had some moves I'm sure none of the others, not even the intimidating teacher, had ever seen.

There she was. I saw Sofia right in the middle of the group of dance students. I could only sneak glimpses of her, June, and the others when they crossed my line of sight through the open door but managed to witness bits and pieces as they made their way through several choreographed numbers. I had to be careful for fear of breaking my concentration and giving the guard a chance to figure out what was going on. Going into our plan, we didn't know which of us would be placed in harm's way, so we each had to be on high alert at all times and stay in sync if we were to get this done. So far so good.

I let the girls at my table take turns practicing some basic moves. They weren't half bad. While they were learning the ins and outs of fancy card dealing, I could keep an eye on June's progress. She was working her way among the dancers, finally positioning herself at Sofia's left side. I had to be careful now. I saw June whisper to Sofia as they executed their dance moves. I needed to be ready at any moment to make our move, but above all else, I couldn't blow my cover.

I stopped my demonstration short when a loud bang startled everyone in the room. This was not a golf cart backfiring or a child dipping into his fireworks stash a few hours early. This was a serious boom and it sounded very close to our location. A commotion outside the front door got all our attention. Two guards were arguing loudly in Russian and it sounded like things were being thrown around. This had to be our cue. I gathered my card girls in a tight circle around the table and spoke to them in my best teacher voice.

"This is the most important American card game that you will learn, so pay close attention girls."

They were very eager students, and listened attentively as I explained the simple steps in Fifty-two Card Pick-up. Our guard chaperone was torn between trying to get a look at what was happening outside and keeping a watchful eye on me and my students. I kept my eye on him until his attention was fully-focused on the front door, then I performed one more flourishing shuffle and let all the cards loose to fly like brightly-winged scorpions into the air around us and float gracefully to the floor. The girls were elated at this ridiculous American game and wholeheartedly scrambled about the floor retrieving the cards and squealing in delight. I used the confusion to drop to my knees and crawl to the hallway in front of the dance practice room where I heard the shrill voices of at least five times as many squealing young women disturbing the somber quiet of the house.

June was helping Sofia to her feet after a fake ankle twist had dropped her to the floor amid exaggerated groans of agony. She ushered the limping Sofia out to the hall while the instructor tried to regain control of her other students. "Over here, June. I think the coast is clear." I moved around and crouched low behind them using their bodies to block the guard's view in case he had given up on the commotions inside and out of the room and realized I was no longer in his custody.

Sticking close together, we slipped into the first room we came to. It was a small bathroom with a window above the toilet just big enough to squeeze through one at a time. June went first. She reached up and guided Sofia's exit through the tiny opening and onto the grass below. I followed without hesitation. We kept to the house, using the ornate shrubbery and landscaping as cover as we made our way around the corner to the back side where we found Michael waiting for us. Nodding once, not saying a word, he led the way back to his small boat and Gunner who stood at attention in the skiff, guarding a neat pile of our discarded belongings including our sensible shoes and my handbag which now contained the clothes I had on before I had transformed into my odd casino dealer/mother hen role.

Michael still hadn't said anything. Back when I first met him, his taciturn manner had been unnerving. But I was more tuned in to his body language now. The crinkles around his eyes spoke just as loud as another person's comments. He found our appearance amusing, to say the least. We must have looked like we were on our way to a masquerade party, but at least at a drama and theater convention, people wouldn't be overly shocked by our appearance. June's shimmery gold dress exposed so much tanned skin it was hard for her to maneuver into a sitting position in the boat and retain some bit of modesty. Her cheeks were turning red, and I was convinced it had more to do with Michael's appreciative stare than the temperature. My own outfit was just as short as hers, but with its flouncy black skirt and large playing card appliques, one was more likely to try to use me for a game of poker than a forbidden sexual encounter. Sofia was wearing a solid black polo shirt with a small red and gold scorpion embroidered above the pocket. Her matching black skirt barely covered her shapely behind, but it was stretchy and she hopped in the boat and sat down like it was part of her daily routine. No one noticed except me.

As we pulled away from Scorpion Island, I could see guards running around like ants, stopping to shield their eyes against the sun, and gazing out into the lake. Our deceivingly simple little skiff fairly flew across the lake, and before the private helicopter had time to take off in our direction, we were once again moored safely at a transient slip in the marina.

As soon as I stepped onto the dock, I saw something that made my heart race and my palms sweat. After executing our plan so flawlessly, how could we have not accounted for this?

Chapter Forty

For you and I are past our dancing days. *~Romeo and Juliet*

June was right behind me and she had seen it too. "They're back, Francie. What time is it?"

"I have no idea. It's not like I had any place to stash my phone in this get-up."

"I know what you mean." June tugged at her hemline to no avail.

Hamm and Jack had returned for the final event of the convention—the murder mystery dinner show June and Eddie and I were so excited to help plan just days ago. I didn't know if they were at the hotel or aboard Lucky Enough which lulled peacefully in its slip. Anyway you looked at it, it wasn't great news.

Michael spoke before I had a chance to worry over the unexpected appearance of our men. "You better get over to the ballroom where the final event is being presented. Don't let Gabriel out of your sight."

"What about Sofia?" I asked. "Should we take her with us? If Gabriel spots her, all hell may break loose."

"A few things still need to happen out here if you want this case closed and the real guilty party exposed. Sofia, will stay back with me. Eddie is getting Sasha up to speed. Go now, and try not to be seen."

Looking down at my oh-so not subtle ensemble, I grabbed June's hand and we headed for the hotel.

Michael had made it clear we didn't have time to go back to our rooms to change into our business casuals, so we held our heads high as we walked through the lobby, ignoring the blatant stares and snickers coming from some of the guests. When we got to the ballroom, I cracked open the door to scope out the layout of the room. The final event was already well underway; it looked like the third course of the four-course sit-down dinner was being served, and everyone's attention was riveted on the actors playing the roles of the ever-changing suspects. Pencils were poised above tickets to make notes of motive, means, and opportunity. There was an impressive prize package to be awarded to the group figuring out the murderer's identity and other specifics of the crime. No one paid the least bit of attention to us as we slunk into a dark corner in the back of the room and sat at a table out of the line of sight of the emcee.

All the players in the real-life murder mystery were in attendance: Gabriel manned the microphone; Damien and Angelina were sitting at at a round table right up front with an empty chair positioned beside each of them; and as luck would have it, the two handsome men rounding out the table for six were none-other than Hamm and Jack. I assumed the two empty chairs were being reserved for me and June.

Detective Reed was seated at the table right next to them looking downright captivating in a soft jade-color linen pantsuit, her strawberry-blond hair brushing her shoulders in soft waves each time she turned her head from side to side, scanning the room for someone or something. I did not recognize the other four people with her. Maybe they were undercover agents, but then again, maybe they were simply hotel guests or conference attendees.

We settled into our shadowy corner to watch Gabriel work his magic. The dinner guests were talking and laughing as they got more and more involved with the interactive presentation. One lady stood up, waving her ticket and squealing in delight as she figured out a connection between two of the actors. Hidden clues were being uncovered with theatrical flourish. Soon the murderer would be revealed.

Amidst the flailing arms and competition to be the first to discover the solution, I saw someone (I couldn't even make out whether it was a man or a woman) lean in close to Detective Reed, whisper something in her ear, and hand her something. The detective looked around the room once again, then down into her lap where she was holding the mysterious delivery, and finally back up, her gaze fixing upon the table right beside her. She stood slowly and made her way toward the DeVilles, Hamm and Jack.

"June, I think something's going down."

"Yeah, I know. We're about to find out who the murderer is. I wish we could have been here for the whole show. This looks like a lot of fun."

"I'm sure it is. I've been to a number of these. I'll sign us up for one in the fall. In the meantime, could you pay attention? Reed is talking to Angelina and Damien. They don't look at all happy."

Hammond and Jack were interjecting questions, but Reed was ignoring them. She got Angelina and Damien to stand up and was directing them to follow her out of the conference room. Two of the strangers who had been with her at her table stood at their places, unmoving, taking in the scene, and making their presence felt.

"We can't let this happen, June. We've got to tell Reed she has the wrong people."

Just then, we both noticed Gabriel who had ditched his microphone and was stealthily making his way toward the nearest door.

"Hey, he's getting away!" June hopped up onto her chair pointing at Gabriel who was trying to slip unnoticed out the service exit.

The crowd loved it. They clapped and shouted with glee as the lady in the short gold dress pointed at the emcee and proclaimed him the murderer from the back of the room. What a grand finale! if only they knew. I mashed my way through the throng trying to make my way to Reed and explain that she had the wrong brother in custody. Across the room, participants blocked Gabriel's way, each one hoping to put the final piece of the puzzle in place and go home with the extravagant prize package.

Bang! Bang! The sound of gunfire brought the crowd to silence in an instance. Gabriel had replaced the discarded mic with a pistol.

The crowd didn't miss a beat. "The smoking gun! How clever! Bravo!"

The room erupted once more, louder and more excited than before. Prior to dinner being served, there would have been a short presentation outlining the structure and rules of the game. It would have been noted, as was the case in every murder mystery dinner I had attended, that guns and other props would be used to make the experience more authentic. The audience cheered at the great performance.

In my heart, I knew those were not blanks being fired. Reed, of course, had recognized them as well, instinctively altering her course in the direction of the gunfire. Angelina and Damien stood at the entrance door June and I had recently used, still guarded by Reed's dinner partners. Static crackled through Detective Reed's radio as she dispatched a call for backup. I was all the way up to the stage area now, close enough to see the look of alarm on my husband's face and witness Detective Jack Morgan spring into action, lurching toward Gabriel, leaving Hamm alone and stunned at the table. I wanted to throw myself into the safety of his arms, but then I'd have to try and explain why I looked as if a deck of giant playing cards had thrown up on me and stolen half my clothes. I kept quiet and hid behind a chair.

From my vantage point, I could see a young man with blood running down the white sleeve of his shirt. Real blood. In a panic, I scanned the room looking for any other casualties, but thank god, I didn't see anyone else injured. Gabriel must have dropped his gun in the crush of humanity vying for their three minutes of fame. I was close enough to see the wild glaze in his eyes. He was trapped in his own game.

By the time Detective Reed reached him, she was joined by four back-up policemen as well as Jack who was standing by in case he could be of assistance.

"Mr. DeVille, calm down, it's over now."

Gabriel growled dangerously, but then he seemed to deflate like a reused party balloon. Gabriel DeVille was taken into custody for inciting panic as well as discharging a firearm illegally, not to mention shooting one of his guests. In the meantime, Angelina and Damien were not being released at the moment. It looked like there would be a DeVille family reunion at the jailhouse tonight.

Chapter Forty-One

Where hast thou been, sister? ~*Macbeth*

After squatting behind that chair for so long, my leg muscles were screaming for release. Hamm had walked off in the direction of the exit, presumably looking for Jack. June was making her way around the perimeter toward me, so deciding the coast was clear, I stood up and did a quick yoga stretch. No one in the theater, except maybe the man who had been shot and whisked away by medical personnel, seemed all too ruffled by the pandemonium. Animated conversation swirled around my head.

"Wow! What a performance!"

"I knew it had to be the emcee. He was too good to be true."

"That gunfire sounded so realistic."

"Did you see the guy with the bloody arm? Now those were some sweet special effects!"

Hard as it was to believe, it seemed the dinner guests had no idea of the actual danger they had all been dragged into by Gabriel's insane scheme. June and I finally reconnected, and only one lady had the nerve to comment on our outfits. "Who are you two supposed to be? Aren't you both a little old for those hemlines?"

"Said the lady with the orange hair," I snickered.

June giggled at my remark. "Right. If I were doing orange, I would have gotten my color out of a box, not a KoolAid packet. But now what? These people are expecting some sort of ending. There were some pretty competitive groups back there. This could get ugly."

"Could? What do you call a guy getting shot and all the owners and coordinators of the event being hauled off to the police station?"

June bit her upper lip. "True. But now they're expecting the winner to be announced."

"And dessert," I added. "I'd be mad if they left out dessert." I got an eye roll from June.

Enter Eddie Sneed. His tuxedo had to have been custom made; you couldn't buy something so tailored and elegant off the rack, at least not in his size. He strode up the main aisle, waving his arms dramatically, the weasel perched above his eyebrows hanging on for dear life. So much for suave and debonair. "Ladies and gentlemen, if you would all take your seats, you will discover the solution to tonight's mystery."

June and I sat down in the seats recently vacated by Hamm and Jack. "This I've got to hear." June whispered. I nodded in agreement. The guests all sat obediently, and an expectant hush fell over the crowd. I had to give the little guy credit. Eddie did a pretty convincing job ad libbing the conclusion of the show, explaining away the crazy guy and the blood and the very real police presence. People nodded in agreement all around the room.

"Aahh, just as I thought."

"Exactly what I had written down." Heads were bowed and pencils frantically scratched out notes on tickets in order to prove the solution had been figured out before the big reveal.

Eddie walked around the room, glad-handing the men and patting the women solicitously on the back or shoulder. After stopping at every table, he made his way back to the podium, picked up the microphone from where it had rolled under a chair during the brouhaha, and announced the grand prize winner. How he determined which group deserved the lavish prize package was beyond me. He probably chose the six people most likely to punch him in the face if they lost.

"Congratulations to our winning group and runners-up! And thank you one and all for being such great sports. Please enjoy your dessert and have a pleasant evening. Don't forget the fireworks at ten o'clock on the beach."

"I told you there should be dessert. Gives the losers something to focus on."

"Okay," June conceded. "Since we're here and no one is trying to kill us at the moment, we might as well stay for a few minutes."

I heard a soft, familiar voice over my shoulder. "Would you prefer the chocolate or the strawberry cheesecake, ma'am?"

For once, her appearance neither startled nor angered me. "Sasha, it's so good to see you. Are you okay? Have you spoken to Eddie about everything that's been happening?"

"I haven't spoken to him since we got to the hotel. There was so much preparation needed for this final act. Now that Gabriel has been arrested, I will be able to breathe a little bit."

Eddie bounded across the room and flung his arms around Sasha. "Oh, Sweetie, there you are. Are you okay?"

"Why does everyone keep asking me that? Of course I'm okay. But what about Sofia? She's the one we need to worry about. I still need to find her."

I couldn't stop the grin that was spreading across my face even if I wanted to. Sofia had approached her sister silently and tapped her on the shoulder.

I was distracted from the exuberant reunion of the sisters by the distinct sound of the ringtone I reserve specifically for Hamm. I didn't have my phone. "What the...?"

Eddie pulled the familiar device from the inner pocket of his tuxedo jacket. "I thought you might be wanting this," he said, handing me my phone.

It was too late to catch the call, but seconds later, a little ping alerted me to the waiting voicemail. "Where are you, Francie? Jack and I came for you guys, but before we could find you, all hell broke loose. You won't believe what just happened, and you'll be sorry you missed all the excitement. Let me know where you are."

I decided to reply via text message to make sure my voice didn't give anything away. In my grammatically correct message, I informed my husband June and I had been working on the show behind the scenes. (True story, right?) Just a little more cleanup to do, and we'd meet back at the boat in about an hour.

Back in our room, changing clothes was our number one priority. I opted for my favorite stretchy black yoga pants and a black and white striped top with a sparkly anchor on the front. The only things I would allow on my feet were my flip flops. I twirled my hair into a loose bun and let the curls around my face land where they would. June must have felt the need to cover all the parts of her body that had been out in the elements far too long. She chose a red and white maxi skirt and a long-sleeved, boat-neck top in navy blue. White ankle socks and red canvas shoes made the outfit uniquely hers.

A knock on the door made me jump, kicking the playing card outfit and shimmery mini dress under the bed as I went for the door.

"May I come in?" Detective Reed said, placing one foot in the doorway. She looked relaxed and more like she was stopping by for a chat among friends than coming to arrest us. What could I say?

"Of course. Please don't mind the mess. We're in the middle of packing. We're leaving the hotel shortly and heading back to the marina for the fireworks. We plan to head home in the morning. That is, well, unless you're here to deliver bad news."

"I think you'll like what I have to say. I had a feeling right from the start you were innocent, Francie. I had to follow the evidence though, and eventually it ended up clearing you of all suspicion. Angelina explained how she had kept your scarf after your visit to her suite. When she learned it was the murder weapon, she didn't know how or if you were involved and kept the information to herself. When Gabriel used the scarf to strangle his brother, he thought it belonged to Angelina.

Angelina and Damien DeVille were also victims in Gabriel's scheme. As soon as they finish up their statements, they will be free to go as well."

"So, about the evidence..." June started.

"A certain man, whose identity I promised not to reveal, presented us with a box full of evidence containing not only everything we needed to charge Gabriel DeVille with murder, conspiracy, kidnapping, and attempted murder, but also links to the Scorpione family and their attempts to take over all of Devil's Island Resort and turn it into a major mob-funded hotbed of gambling and other activities completely against the values and lifestyle of our lake town residents. There was also evidence that Bob had been involved in some shady dealings of his own on a much smaller scale. The police department owes both of you our sincere apologies. I hope you don't leave with bad feelings."

June called the front desk to collect our bags and deliver them to our dock. Without a backward glance, we stepped into the hall, and I shut the door behind us for the last time.

Chapter Forty-Two

All's Well That Ends Well

Hamm and Jack were ready for us. The smell of hot pepperoni pizza greeted us even before we stepped aboard. There was a bottle of wine, uncorked and waiting to be poured into real glass stemware. "Welcome back, ladies. We can't wait to hear all about your weekend."

"There's nothing much to tell. You've probably heard the same stories from me a hundred times." I smiled sweetly at Hamm.

"There were some pretty cool zombies at lunch one day," June chimed in.

"How could I forget? Oh, and I got to play magician's assistant on stage."

Hamm smiled and humored me. "We enjoyed what we saw of the final dinner show."

"I must confess," Jack added, "they had me fooled. I was up and ready to help the cops catch a crook, but was informed by a short guy in a tuxedo and a bad toupee that it was all part of the grand finale."

"Why don't you tell us about your weekend instead. It was probably much more interesting." They both took the bait.

For the next half hour June and I pretended to be fascinated by their stories of birdies, holes-in-one, and hijinx on the golf greens. Yawn.

The moon shone through the cloudless sky and reflected in the mirror of the lake. It was a perfect night. We were anchored off shore and the fireworks were about to begin. After indulging in a second glass of wine, I curled up next to Hamm in the sweet comfort of his warm embrace to wait for the show.

"Fantastic! That was the best fireworks display I've ever seen." Jack hopped up and pumped his fist in the air, causing the boat to list to the starboard side.

"Huh?" I sat up and rubbed my eyes. "Did I miss something?"

Hamm kissed my forehead and tucked a fuzzy blanket around my shoulders before starting up the engines and heading for Beacon Pointe. Fifteen minutes later we were back in our own slip across the bay.

Finis

The rich aroma of my favorite coffee enticed me from my sleep, and I followed my nose out to the kitchen of our condo where Hamm sat holding a mug and reading the morning news. Cup in hand, I joined him at the table. I was still relishing my first sip, when Hamm set the carefully folded newspaper on the table so I could see the lead story. A full-color photo of Gabriel DeVille in handcuffs graced half the front page. Under the picture ran the headline, "Murder, Mayhem and Mafia Star at Drama Divas Convention."

I read the first few lines of the story and felt the color rising in my cheeks. "The dynamic duo strikes again keeping our peaceful Lake Erie islands and shores free from criminal activity..."

"Is there anything you would like to tell me about, Dear?"

Don't miss out!

Visit the website below and you can sign up to receive emails whenever Olivia Breen publishes a new book. There's no charge and no obligation.

https://books2read.com/r/B-A-QENN-TGFMB

BOOKS 2 READ

Connecting independent readers to independent writers.

Also by Olivia Breen

Lake Erie Mysteries
Sunny Side Up
Deviled
Scrambled

www.ingramcontent.com/pod-product-compliance
Lightning Source LLC
Chambersburg PA
CBHW050323160726
48002CB00001B/155